Echoes o

A Book of Contrasts by the
Brighton NightWriters

Published in Great Britain 2024 by Brighton NightWriters

Editor: Tim Shelton-Jones

Cover artwork: Alanna MacIntyre (adapted by Tim)

Copyright © the authors, all rights reserved

ISBN: 9798378399789

Printed by: Kindle Direct Publishing

**Brighton NightWriters have been meeting once a week since 1988 to discuss members' work in a friendly, supportive atmosphere. Some of us have been attending since the beginning, others are complete newcomers; some attend regularly, others irregularly.
All are welcome.**

NightWriters meets at the Manor Road Gym, Manor Rd, Brighton BN2 5EA every Wednesday at 7.30pm.

New writers are always welcome. Just come along or contact Tim Shelton-Jones on 01273 505642 for more information.

Visit us at: ***https://brightonnightwriters.wordpress.com/***

+ our Facebook page at: *facebook.com/brightonnightwriters*

CONTENTS

    In Memoriam David Benedictus   5

    Introduction and Acknowledgements   7

1 Melanie Bell   9

2 Joao de Sousa   13

3 Nick Wild   27

4 Rodney Cunningham   39

5 Mike Harmer   51

6 David Benedictus   63

7 Enzo Marra   67

8 Libby Proe   69

9 Leila Bendimered   73

10 Debbie Waldon   76

11 Mark Burrow   82

12 Niall Drennan   104

13 Marita Wild   116

14 Aidan Hopkins   119

15 Alanna McIntyre   124

16 Tim Shelton-Jones   126

17 Rod Watson   139

    (more overleaf)

18	Tony Frisby	149
19	John Holmes	156
20	Kathie Wilson	170
21	B	174
22	Heather Clavering	186
23	Paul G Terry	192
24	Dee Johnson	195
25	Matthew Shelton-Jones	203
26	Gus Watcham	207

In Memoriam David Benedictus
11th September 1938 – 4th October 2023

David was a long-standing and dedicated member of the group. His writing, his witty contributions, and his sheer presence, are greatly missed

Introduction

Welcome to Echoes of Light, the ninth anthology of the Brighton NightWriters. With 26 contributors, Echoes of Light offers a richly varied selection of prose and poetry from some of the city's most talented and original writers. Learn all about Brighton's long-lost subversive bookshop, the Unicorn, lauded by Graham Greene and rescued from legal expenses by its customers, including Allen Ginsberg. Or just sit back and watch "Clouds like gangsters / Threatening the Sun".

The book's theme – 'Dark and light' – weaves its way in and out of these pages. Some pieces have been written to the theme, others not, and it is left to the reader to discover for him/herself where the light shines and when it lies hidden.

The order of appearance of authors was determined by random number generator. Author biographies, where submitted, appear after each author's contributions.

Happy reading!

And if you like what you see and wonder if there is more – yes, there always is, and you can be part of it by joining the Brighton NightWriters, *currently meeting on Wednesday evenings at 7.30pm in the Manor Road Gym. More details can be found on our website https://brightonnightwriters.wordpress.com, or just ring me (Tim Shelton-Jones) on 07747 301706.*

Reviews

Do feel free to leave a review of Echoes of Light on Amazon (google "NightWriters Echoes of Light"), where you can also order more copies.

Acknowledgements

Thanks go to Alanna McIntyre for her artwork, which appears on the front and back covers. Thanks also to our editors Debbie Waldon, Mark Burrow and Tim Shelton-Jones, and to Tim Shelton-Jones for compiling and producing the book. And finally, very many thanks go of course to NightWriters' members for freely contributing their work to Echoes of Light.

Picking Hazelnuts with the Devil
by Melanie Bell

She didn't want to marry him, but she'd said she would. It would secure her future. Her family liked him, this promising young shipbuilder. A good man. Gentle.

Emma was bored with gentle. She wanted to dance in the storm. To eat cake before dinner. To try out a lover or two, and not just the one she'd been promised, soft-voiced Sam who spoke to her in ums and ahs and stared at her like a sleepy calf.

There wasn't much excitement to be had in her town. She was only 19. She wanted some.

All her life, she'd heeded the folktales and refused to do the things they advised against. The wedding was in a week, tension closing in like a noose around her neck. She couldn't speak without wanting to sob. Her mother teased her about the healthy children she'd bear and how fine she'd look in her wedding gown.

It was Sunday, graced with a sky as clear as glass. Warning words circled her mind. She didn't know what made her do it; whether an imp dwelt in her heart.

"I'm going out for a walk, Mum."

She grabbed a basket.

"Be back soon."

And as simple as that, she was out.

All those years of minding her studies, minding her manners, minding her elders. Why hadn't she done this before?

Emma skipped down the woodland path to the hazel

tree, waving to the knobbly old men she passed. In the heart of the woods, there was no one. She stood under the branches and fluffed out her skirts.

The hazelnuts were ripe. She began to gather one of her favourite snacks. Her cousins had a hazel tree and harvested the nuts in the fall. They'd all be at her wedding, smiling, while she smiled back like a painted doll.

Questions swirled like wind: Why didn't she want that? And, following briskly on its heels: Did *anyone* want that?

A shadow crept behind her. Hairs prickled on the back of her hands.

She heard heavy footsteps, and a man's voice singing a hearty tune. One with no words, only nonsense sounds. A great baritone, like in the opera.

Oh, if she could sing…

Her head turned, following the voice.

He was handsome, that was sure. Handsome, and not human at all. He wore a vest made of fur, and not much else. Long hair hung plaited down his back. Two horns stuck out atop his head like thorns. A grin twisted his face.

"Hello, beautiful thing," he said.

Emma was not used to the type of attention that lit his face. The golden eyes that locked on hers, dancing and sparkling like firelight.

Her plan had worked. Someone had come to meet her. Whether this was the right fellow or not, Emma couldn't say, but she found she didn't much care.

"Um. Hello." The quaver in her voice would hide her intentions nicely.

"May I know your name?" he asked.

She knew not to tell one's true name to the fairies, but this wasn't a fairy, was he? Besides, she could tell him only what people called her. Properly, it was her middle name, following the saint's, and her last name, even if he knew it now, was about to change.

"I'm Emma."

"Are you?"

He peered at her with inquisitive eyes. Of course, it was within the devil's power to stare into one's very soul.

"You can certainly call me that." She wondered at the smile crossing her face, the playful rise of air in her chest. Was she teasing him?

"Pleased to know you. I have been granted many names by many parties, but 'the devil' should do." Emma's heart thudded. *So it's true.* She was afraid, but not only that. Also curious. Also eager. Ready to take a bite out of the world.

The devil bowed at the waist. He extended a hand, claw-tipped and calloused. Emma went to shake it. Instead, he raised her hand to his lips and kissed the back of it. It was not a soft kiss but a roguish one.

Emma grabbed his hand, pulling as if in a tug-of-war. She kissed it back, remembering children dancing and chanting in rings, recalling the song her people only half believed:

"If hazelnuts on Sunday you pluck,
be wary of what you'll find.
The devil shall creep up on you
and take you from behind.
On your wedding day you'll carry his kin
if you dare let the devil in!"

Emma could be a devil, too.

"Ah," he grinned, revealing fangs. "So that's how you like to play!"

She did not know the steps to this dance. But oh, how she wanted to! She followed, letting him pull her close, place a hand around her waist. Her stomach quivered. She relished the roughness of his touch, so different from her fiancé's temperament (at least so far; it occurred to her now that they'd never touched). And they lay together under the hazel tree, nuts spilling from the basket, forgotten.

Emma's family ate hazelnuts that Sunday, and she married with a sly smile. The good girl had a secret now. She could steer the ship herself.

Emma's first child was born just under nine months after her wedding, too late for anyone to know. They named her firstborn Samantha, after her husband. She did not resemble Sam. She looked human enough, but as she grew, it became clear she carried mischief in her heart. She liked to eat worms and spill milk, though Emma's mum said that's just what babies did, and her little voice sounded like music.

"She takes after you," her mother smiled, feeding her granddaughter a hazelnut.

Melanie Bell *is the author of* Chasing Harmony, Dream Signs, *and* The Modern Enneagram. *Her work has appeared onstage at London's Tower Theatre and in print in publications such as* Cossmass Infinities, Contrary, *and* The Fiddlehead. *A Canadian living in the UK, she loves art, music, wondering, and wandering.*

Zen Vibes
by Joao de Souza

Take the road

No end in sight

No bother. Each step a discovery

Each passerby a friend to be

Do not look back too often

Just make sure each step is steady

Each error registered for prevention.

As the day progresses

The light bathes the fruit trees

That feed you

Do not long for the night;

It will allow you to rest,

And then

You may revert to dreams.

Untitled
by Joao de Souza

My female condition?
But that is men's language.
All human-hood is always about men.

Still when you ceased,
all to me is left.
You are now gone. I'm released.
Your shelter, your shield,
your name upon my name ...
the gates that you closed
are now open ajar,
life starts now
and I, I am the main star.

Thanks for all your gifts.
The best just came:
life is an opportunity
now that you left the game.

Dark
by Joao de Souza

dark, socially unacceptable thoughts

forcing to deviate from accepted normality,

self-pity,

the despair of social inadequacy,

just another victim of self confusion

and rotten standards of normality

in the cover of night

his visions robbed him of sleep and rest

and found no net where to take refuge,

no friend to confide

nor lovers to share his shame

and feast on a joined journey

with silent, shameless pride

and so his life was such a lost game

another defeat he had to hide

Day light - *The dark side of the morning*
by Joao de Souza

Some days you may wake up
eyes fully closed

an automat, you carry your chores
for you were told
that was the right thing to do
duty wise

some nights you sleep with dreams wide awake
projecting the future built on past experiences
but most of the time your robotic moves
avoid the burden of freedom and choice

automatic pilot, inner conformism,
"is gonna be alright" dumb attitude

and other days you write
as some cleansing of guilt that your fantasy courts
you fear the day when the end will knock
and no strength is available to shut the door

as the torrent of disease wrecks body and spirit

and eternal night settles
before you could touch the truth of life

for life's meaning is nowhere to find

you dig, you search, you think, revise,
make judgements, find no conclusions
only anguish and anger in your mind remain

you are, you've been, another speck of dust
on this pathetic landscape of human stain

why are we here, you keep asking
where to go now, and who, what, takes me wherever

am I awake or dead
is the lasting dream this nightmare
why have I been here

this ignorance is, surely, not fair
I'm covered in questions
that breed more doubts
and, honestly, not anymore,
from now on, sorry, really sorry,
for I miss the strength,
and I no longer dare,
and I no longer care.

The Widow's song
by Joao de Souza

I find myself under this sunshine

projecting your shadow,

thinking your thoughts,

your heavy hand still upon me

the keys of my home,

the windows of the mind

you drag them with you,

my eyes are transfixed

my being still yours.

Was that love, that bounded us?

Yours was the alpha voice,

your hands on the helm

that drove our lives,

I've been following your shadow ...

Would you leave me now

return my freedom

release me from you?

Sorrows
by Joao de Souza

Do not apologise for your sins

no one ever has had a clean hand

nor a non-dirty mind, from start to end.

Atonement for conditions we've been immersed in

and that led us to commit faults and crimes,

which side of God's nature

moulded us this badly

which platoon of Angels slept

as you let flow your wronged mind,

direct you to harm, to shame,

to hate, to crime ... ?

Absolution, penitence, penance,

all this solid religious guilt,

let it go, move on, shake it off,

throw to the wind the carried burden,

hide all your wrongdoings,

extend your friendly hand to hopeless beings,

kindle a flickering flame of hope in their minds and settings ...

make love constantly to others,

with extended hands, a smile, a sandwich perhaps,
or a cigarette and beer ...
do not judge the poor, just stay there,
inhale the acrid scent of unwashed clothes and skin.
How lucky you have been this far
able to be, to stay, or to become a presentable human being
Procrastination is a waste,
your time, as mine too, is fleeing.

Untitled
by Joao de Souza

How long
I will still be here

it is no to defeat,
no capitulation
the world has no cure
nor have for its wrongs
the solutions

the trees talk to me
their silence is love
they will stay here
long after I am gone
they've seen many come,
pass by
disappear
they seem to murmur

"Have no fear"

this October day I smile,
I do smile
the fear eloped with familiar demons
I'm happy, I write,
but sad of my limits,
can't pass what I know

So I write and share
these thoughts that arise
while listening to nature

maybe
maybe you can sit, not still but attentive

Here and now
by Joao de Souza

Here I am

sitting on 'my' park bench

waiting for words to cascade and make sense

giving them life

then march in parade

though on a wrong compass

multiple cadences

forget uniformity and norms

leave them hanging from the fence

who reads me can imprint the rhythm,

music, cadence,

renewed in each reading

the poem must sit silent

an orchestra with no conductor,

it never repeats its message for it avoids ageing

here the green leaves of perennial trees

and golden autumn leaves

fallen from now naked trunks;

looking dried, small branches reach to the skies

to me make me feel lucky and happy

as mortal humans can be

when a child passes, it is the future looming

an energetic dog waves the tail to me,

as a welcome and a good bye,

then runs away from this brief while

as his life span is shorter

than the one in me

the clouds cover the sky,

the mood is grey,

train stays away, it is lunch hour, there are no children
 present

I come from the past

and enjoy this relative calm

wondering how long

This does not pretend to be a Poem
by Joao de Souza

Drops of rain tickling on the window

A quiet wind blowing on tree branches.

The birds quietened

the water running down, licking feathers,

their open eyes staring, with no motion.

Grey light flown down from veiled skies

the street is almost still, no walkers passing by,

wipers on incoming bus shields seem to shake heads saying softly: "No, No"

while the tyres rub the asphalt on wet splashes.

Winter scene on a betrayed Spring day.

Buildings and trees are clearly lined on our vision field

the pavement shining, wet, as sadness settles down our eyes.

End of morning. Wait for caffeine to take over.

Night dreams and mares exhausted the imagination.

No ideas to scratch out of the mind.

Monday isn't a start, just a carbon copy

of previous days embedded in boredom.

There is, on other streets, a vibe of passions and dramas,

shoppers busy buying into their neutered lives:

Sports, politics, love affairs, innovations and decay,

us all running nowhere

while life's cycles stay inconstant,

Trying to keep quiet looking at the window,

deprived of ideas, no philosophy to apply,

I stare

the fluidity of thoughts like a painting gallery

with strong brush strokes and dark corner spots.

I let the contours spring from my imagination

out of idleness, this almost pleasant feeling of blunt

spice-less life of mediocrity

drawing non poetic lines ad infinity.

Awareness is Dark
by Nick Wild

You step inside the void.

Stars illuminate the night sky.

Lost in the vacuum of space, out of reach, in another dimension.

A new candle burns.

I search the heavens for you.

The transience of being.

In an awakened state of mind.

Nothing remained, senses deranged.

Touch and taste were numb, eyes were blind, your scent had gone.

Clock ticked, time passed slowly.

Stray dog howled to the full moon.

I become aware again.

Skeletal trees sway together in silent winds.
Birds are quiet, roosting.
Streets are haunting and empty, lit by acid hued lights.
Nightmares are approaching.
Cats prowl in alleyways.

Will I ever find you again?

Shrouded in dust, books piled up.
Ideas submerged.
Thoughts were bleak, I couldn't speak, a silhouette of myself.
My mind was empty.
No essence of me remained.

Words began to form again.

Bed was a refuge.
Walls entombed me.
Twisted gnarled oak creaked. I ceased to exist.
The desolation peaked.
Were you lost forever?

I begin to dream again.

Your presence is eternal.
Embrace the darkness.
Let it inspire you. Wild eyes hidden by mask.
Don't run from your shadow.
Allow it to follow and protect you.

I begin to hope again.

The hope grows.
Leaves unfurl.
Plants rise from the earth, they start to move and dance.
The sun shines.
New life is born.

The world begins to breathe again.

Narcissus gazes into mirrored pool.
Echo calls out his name.
Vibrations ripple across the water, his reflection shimmers.
A flower blooms.
The dissolution of self.

Angels begin to sing again.

Awareness is universal,
awareness is creation,
awareness is nothing,
awareness is energy,
awareness is infinite,
awareness is chaos,
awareness is divine,
awareness is being,
awareness is dark,
awareness is light.

Awareness is reawakening.

Again I smell your scent.
You appear before me.
Spirit softly glowing, your soul set free, gently smiling.
We begin to speak.
I reach out to touch you.

Thunder Clouds
by Nick Wild

Thunder clouds are gathering;

the air is cooling;

a breeze is building.

Bees are busily collecting pollen

from wild geraniums before the rains come.

Purple hues, from light to dark,

their delicate blooms proliferate the garden.

The process of florescence.

Blushing roses, buds newly opened,

scarlet red – colour gently glowing,

beautiful and perfectly formed.

The sky is darkening.

A lazy Sunday afternoon, quietly pottering,

pondering, dead heading,

getting ready for the storm.

Anticipating the impending downfall,

my neighbour unpegs the washing

from the line in her garden.

Eagerly awaited, a long time coming.

It's been nearly two months now.

Soothing sounds of water droplets
start to fall onto the leaves of the elm tree,
dripping down and quenching the dry grass beneath.
The earthly smell of fresh summer rain,
revitalising the parched dry ground,
puddles forming on concrete yard.
Plants seem to smile happily,
knowing, sensing and energised.
The deluge refreshes naked skin,
cleansing the soul,
bare feet connected to the damp earth,
grounding me.

The Rats
by Nick Wild

And in my mind I spoke to you so many times…

trains pass behind the blinds; naked damson tree stands by crumbling flint wall.

Flames flickered in fire place of glowing embers.

Midnight calls and red wine chimes.

Later, church bells ring and the blackbird begins to sing a new dawn chorus.

It's not the end, it's the start of a new day;

music always plays and memories remain,

an era of crazy times, beat up rhymes

and when the lights go out the railway lines still rumble;

you sleep and I stumble to bed again...

Another time and I listen to the silence.

And in the solitude hear

the rats that tinker with my mind.

Black Dog of Depression
by Nick Wild

The black dog follows me, he knows where I go

and every time I run from him, he bites me on the toe.

Sometimes I can hide, but I never really know

when he's going to spring up on me, or if he'll ever
 let me go.

The black dog's not my friend, he's ugly and he growls

and when he takes a hold of me, he listens to my howls.

And next time that he follows me, I'll kick him in
 the guts;

if that doesn't do the trick, I'll twist his fucking nuts.

Attack of the Scale Insects
by Nick Wild

Monday 29 May 2023

08:17

Another bank holiday; a day off from work.

I wonder if I can still actually write. I haven't been to NightWriters for a while. I haven't written for a while, although looking at my desk I must have done; it's covered in A4 white paper all filled up with my scrawl. So I've been writing something, various bits, but have I got the energy, focus or drive to finish anything? I don't even know what I've started. More fragments, but fragments of what? A book, a story? Maybe a character profile, maybe several. But the problem is when I look at the pieces of paper they just jumble up, the words stumble, I fumble trying to grasp something, anything, shuffling the pages. Maybe I should mess them up. Cut them up. Screw up the whole lot of them.

Sometimes I think I'm not in the mood to write, not feeling dark enough, nothing to say, no words to conjure. I need a muse to amuse me, someone to think about, to relate to, rebound off, or a catastrophe, an alarm, something to arrest my senses.

But no, I just have to do it. Not be precious, not be… Just be… Just be aware, be present in this moment, to not be scared; allow a waver in the stream of thought. Write without looking back. An unconscious flow, a river of words, crashing into the banks, eddying in pools, forcing its way through, carving rock and morphing steel, being free. Water is an entity, an energy. Water is alive.

Outside the sun shines, a seagull squarks, the sky is blue and the leaves and boughs of trees dance in the wind. Roses are blooming, one red with a pink blush, another deep velvet red, shadows blackened. The vegetable plot is finally weeded. At last, I cleared the borage, bindweed, grass and dandelions. All that's growing in it now is a sweet musky rosemary tree, strawberry plants from the year before, surviving, with small delicate white flowers dotted yellow. The chard has survived too. The snails and slugs left it alone and it continues to grow. The white chard looks mutated with a twisted stem, two feet tall. Ferrules giving it strength. Will leave it and see what develops. Maybe trim some off and roast it. With a little oil and salt, in a hot oven, it soon dries out and becomes crispy like dried seaweed.

The blackcurrant bush has also survived and is looking healthy for the first time in a few years. It suffered a scale insect attack last year. Little nodules, brown, black spots, like growths on the branches, especially the older branches. They are clever little insects; they create a community, little single dwellings, all grouped together, from near the base of the branches to the mid-section. They only seem to grow on old wood, camouflaged against the bark. You can pick them off like a scab and it was quite satisfying doing so, but without the itching feeling of relief you get on skin, or the slight pain when the scab's not ready. So picking the scales off was amusing, but futile. There were too many of them by the time I noticed them and identified what they were.

Their lifecycle is interesting. The little insect builds his cave, his nodule, under which to hide, to be protected from the hot sun, from predators, from ladybirds. Inside his lair sap is sucked from the branches. If you had just a few scale insects you'd never notice, but my blackcurrant was so infested the leaves were being distorted, pulled out of shape like the leaves I can see blowing in the trees right now. It was the mutant leaves that drew my attention and on closer inspection I noticed them. So they damage the leaves, suck the sap and the yield of the fruit is significantly reduced. In fact, last year I got hardly any berries at all.

After much research of how to remedy the problem, such as rubbing infected branches with an alcohol soaked rag, spraying the plant with an insecticide, a pesticide, which I don't like to do, I want my blackcurrants to remain organic, free from poisonous chemicals. I certainly don't want to kill off any other little bugs. I like bugs and they are important ecologically to the locality.

Anyway, not to ramble on, I decided on a hard prune of my blackcurrant bush, much to the displeasure of the ant colony which had already begun its honeydew farm. I think they work in symbiosis with the scale insects, feeding off the sticky sweet residue they create. I certainly didn't want to destroy the ant colony that had been building up.. Ants are so clever, they also farm aphids, greenfly or black fly for the same reason; they reap the harvest of honeydew which they eat to their delight.

So I pruned back any wood that was infected with these pesky varmints, which also opened up the plant, allowing light into the centre of it. I probably won't get much of a crop this year as the fruit forms on the last year's growth, although it has flowered, so I seem to have some berries starting to form, maybe enough for a pie. I hope so; my son and I both love blackcurrant pie.

A blue tit just made an appearance in the garden. The first new bird I've seen in there for a while. Ok, so it was just a blue tit, nothing special, but to me it was. I've seen a robin, a pair of blackbirds (one of whom is singing now), Dave the Seagull, a few doves and some magpies, but never a blue tit. There are some swifts nesting in the eaves of the roof at the front of the house as well. Rebecca, who lives upstairs, told me about them last week; I still haven't actually seen them yet. So the birds are starting to return to the garden, now that the local cats seem to have mysteriously relocated.

I'm feeling happy. At the moment that's the only way I can describe it. It's like there's a new warmth in my heart. It feels unfamiliar, slightly alien to me; it's weird. Nothing has happened. Everything is just the same as yesterday, last week, last month; it's strange to have this feeling. I've been busy in the garden, maybe it's because of a closer connection to nature or that I've been keeping myself active, amused, feeling alive. The sun is shining and the birds are singing.

And I've started to write again.

Nothing special. Not about anything in particular, just writing.

I don't know, life just feels good again.

Maleism
by Rodney Cunningham

Back in the day
I wrote, performed
On stages, streets
On boulevards
I find myself today
Performing at Shine so Hard
I thought I had seen, heard,
Experienced it all
Maybe that's just my Maleism

I saw her take the stage
I thought she was pretty
Let us pay attention
To what she has to say
The poetry she read
Was original very real
Not at all pretentious
Not at all fake

She was smart confident
Without any mistakes
The Maleism inside me
Began to shake

I could tell she was a feminist

Her words expressed
Sorrow beauty and rage
My Maleism said
"Man you don't have a chance
This woman is experienced
She won't dance your kind of dance"

From that moment on
The war of thoughts
Began its battle
My Maleism trembled
My heart began to rattle
In this battle of the Sexes
I remain a pacifist
But if I tell her I like her
She may take offence
She is definitely a feminist
Her poetry is intense
I'll just remain quite
Pass into past tense
If Love is meant to be
Time will tell without pretence.
She was so smart
And confident.

Cloud Watching
by Rodney Cunningham

Clouds like ghosts of white

Against the blue sky

Clouds like gangsters

Threatening the Sun

Water in the sky

Floating on high

The sky wants to cry

No tears yet

Just hovering pent up emotions

Flying floating

Not sure if they want to explode

Or just colour the day grey

Little fluffy Clouds!

Belief
by Rodney Cunningham

Belief kills
Belief cures
Whatever you believe
Becomes true
For you
Be careful what you wish for
Not everything in life is meant to be yours
No one knows what is behind the closed door

I believe in the creator of creativity
I believe in the beauty of simplicity
I believe in poetic creative energy

If you believe in chasing shallow thrills
If you are constantly on the move
Never in the still
The what you believe
Will surely kill
If you believe in yourself
Yet remain in the humble
Remain in the pure
Then what you believe will surely cure....

Mounting Two Horses
by Rodney Cunningham

With your schools and your concert halls
With your churches and your shopping malls
With your cars and your feet
With your gardens and your streets
With your newspapers and Bibles
With your lovers and your idols
With your judgement and your pardons
With soft feelings that are hardened
With your women and your men
With your beginning and your end

Mounting two horses every day
We get so carried away
By all the choices
The choices and voices in my head
By all the voices
The voices and choices in my head
Falling down falling down
And being dragged around
In the dust of the ground
We are being dragged around

Confusion is illusion
Ride one horse
To the finish line
of LIFE....

Conceit
by Rodney Cunningham

I eat with conceit

"Excuse me take this back now

This champagne is too sweet"

"Sorry Sir I'll be right back"

"WHERE IN THE DAMN HELL ARE YOU GOING?"

"To the toilet sir"

"Who said you can do that?

Not me I am the aristocrat

You will go when I tell you

I am power

Now sit Up little girl

Your tears I will not wipe

Type, type, type Damn it!"

"Sorry Sir I am about to explode"

"Funny that is I want that for myself and the WORLD

Sorry what is your name again?"

The Money
by Rodney Cunningham

It all Comes down to the Money
Like the energy of electricity
The fuel of Life
Where would you be
Without the Sunrise
Painting Colours in the Sky
Painting Flowers on Earth
How good is your Garden?
How much did you pay for it
Too look like that?

Like your Car
Like your home
Whatever entertainment you choose
Or places to roam
As you walk alone
Suddenly you realise
As another child dies
Give me a Cheese Burger & Fries
I may put on weight
Exercises in lies

As you are mentally raped by whatever
They choose to Advertise ?
As fake as the Actor in costume
Televised lies
Beaming through your
Living room
"Would you like Champagne
Or Coffee honey?"
Just remember

That it all comes down to
THE MONEY!

Nothing
by Rodney Cunningham

"Nothing from nothing from nothing
Leaves nothing
You've got to have something
If you want to be with me
No romance without finance"

All of this sounds like
Legalised prostitution to me
Why should I pay for your love?
Are you Madonna the "Material girl"
Living in a material world?
Do I have to pay for your autograph as well?
How about I just pay for your signature
On our divorce papers instead?
I have nothing
Therefore I am nothing to you
I will have to learn nothing too

There is no such thing as nothing

Even nothing is something

Empty is plenty with space to share

Empty can be gentle

Still nothing to you

Is what I am meant to be

I have nothing

I am nothing

That within itself

Is really quite something

So if I am nothing to you

I will learn to love nothing too

When I hear nothing

I hear silence

I hear the violence of thought

At war with what I've been taught

Which is I am Nothing to you

So I will love nothing too.....

Anniversary
by Rodney Cunningham

I was alone
I had been alone for years
Even in company I was alone
Lonely were my tears
I was alone within my fears
I was worry

Then she walked through the door
She was quick, fast and in a hurry
At first sight I knew I'd be alone no more
I had never seen anyone like her before
We both smiled
More than once or twice
Then we shook hands
Her skin felt so nice
Maybe because I was so alone
I would have to pay a price?
But her love was for free
To my satisfied glee
Thank you dear Charlotte
I wish us both
A Happy Wedding Anniversary ...

Shame
by Rodney Cunningham

I will take it to my grave
The shame of a generation
We remain still enslaved
To the rose of power
That built this so-called country
The truth I have to tell
As a poet! It is my duty
To seek Beauty in the pain

I live above it
Exorcise the Lies
As I fly through the skies
Truth is amphibious
Water air water
The Sunshine of compromise
Tan your skin
I don't have to tan mine

We are beyond colours anyway
Now would you like a glass of
Red or White Wine?

Done For
by Mike Harmer

Jackie came downstairs with a bucket. Dirty green water was everywhere. Sea defences in Lowleigh-on-Sea were to be reinforced last autumn. Nothing happened.
Andrew thought Lowleigh would be their lifetime home. Now sewage lapped at their ankles.

In the bay, desperate men in gum boots waded beside red danger flags. They dug for oysters, shovelled them into sacks.

Sluices and outlet pipes spewed scum and stench. The Water Company reported no sea walls breached and minimal threats to village or marine life.

The sun set. Oil on water. 'Look, Daddy! The sea is on fire.' Andrew held their son tight. Water was rising.

Loudspeakers crackled: 'Danger...Keep off sea walls.' Red lights flickered from distant ships.

A teddy bear floated face down. Jackie said: 'Andrew - we can't live here anymore.'

The rising tide breached the sea wall. Effluent and sludge swept across Lowleigh's cobbled streets. Stench was everywhere.

They started to pack. Up to their knees in sewage. Car keys were futile. From the upper bedroom, Lowleigh's first climate refugees shouted for help.

Andrew held their son. Jackie banged the bucket. TV cameras arrived in boats.

Dark and Light
by Mike Harmer

'Dark and light: you can't have them both at the same time. Can you? I mean, really, it's not possible is it? In the light, you can see. In the dark you can't see. But if it's too bright, you can't see either....So are they opposites? What would Kant say about these categories? What would Kant say about sex?'

That's what I wrote on the back page of the Rough Guide. But it was dark. I mumbled. I drowsed. We were on a night coach crossing Europe to Turkey and Asia.

Cyllene said wearily 'They are not opposites, Marty, but cousins' and her head rolled away from my shoulder. 'Don't get so binary. Night, day. Black, white. Woman, man. Gay, straight. Just so typical.'

'I thought you were asleep' I yawned.

'I was, but Marty! *You* were talking in your sleep. Again. You woke me up. I wish I'd taken that night boat now. Those yanks were the lively guys.'

I had no words left. Leaving Europe behind. This journey together was going nowhere.

Cyllene yawned, wrapped her scarf around her neck. The flash of a passing lorry illuminated her smooth cheeks. She closed her eyes. There were four rings on her fingers. One of them from me. I touched her hand. There was a feint odour of Patchouli. Her black hair covered her face like a mask. She pressed her body against the coach window, away from me.

So, I got it. Now the distances had begun. Despite what happened on the ferry. We will not be sharing contact details.

I gazed out of the window on the other side of the coach. The intimacy of night. A black desert. On street corners and motorway junctions, embers glowed in barrels. Old men gnawed meat, smoked cigarettes, discarded them, kicked the butts into the kerb and stamped on them.

You meet people, don't you? On these trips, I mean, it all flashes bright. Excitement. Desire. Closeness. Then it dribbles away to nothing. Now, neither the landscape, nor the city, nor even the lights mattered anymore.

The driver changed gears noisily. The Blue Mosque turned black in the distance. The call to prayers had ended. A man snored from the seat behind me. Cyllene was fast asleep in the dark coach: next to me, far from me. In a kind of category Kant can't see.

I will change coaches at the next terminus, before sunlight, when it will still be dark. Then I will never see Cyllene again.

Men Talking
by Mike Harmer

'OK, but Terresa who?'

'You know, Terresa, Terresa Jules.'

'Never heard of her.'

'Of course you have, you idiot! Terresa! Terresa Jules!'

'Remind me, Martin.'

'Terresa – the woman wearing lots of colours! Jewels and jewellery! Travelled round the world.'

'Doesn't ring a bell, matey!'

'So Bob, you've never heard of 'campanology'?

'Ah, yeah, like the art of camping?'

'No, you arsehole. I am talking about bells. A bad joke. Forget it. Terresa lives opposite the old church.'

'Ah religious bells then. Martin! I didn't know you were that sort?'

'No. Just a bad joke! But Terresa is an amazing woman.'

'Ah hah'

'Bob! She's got an amazing car, maybe that jogs your

cynical memory?'

'A Ford?'

'No. It's a Mazda MX 5. Sports de lux. Red all over. Built like a tank. And it's a convertible. That's her style.'

'Ah, now you're talking! What's the serial number. I'll look it up. What year is it?'

'Bob! I am talking about Terresa, not the bloody car. I never asked her about the bloody year!

'Sounds like it's bloody red.'

'Yes, bloody almighty strong, built like a tank, purrs like a tiger.'

"Is that the woman or the car that purrs, Martin?'

'Bob! Wake up! We're talking about the car. But actually you were. I was talking about this amazing woman called Terresa. Remember?'

'Ah yeah, so Martin, what did you say she was called? Jewel?

'No that's what she wears! She's called Terresa. Terresa with two 'r's in it.'

'Ah huh. So what's she into then? Apart from fast cars and bell ringing?

'Huh! Blimey, Bob, you're hard work, very hard bloody work. How about getting on with fixing the window frames.'

'Hand me a No 7. Yeah, that's it – on top of the wrench.'

'So you split up with your squeeze, Bob?'

'Ah hah, yeah, yeah. Karen? High maintenance. But we keep in touch.'

'What? The windows or your ex?'

'Hah. Hah. Hah. At least I can go down the pub when I want. But I wouldn't mind it if she came.'

'Well, me too. We often go to the Red Lion together. It's fun. She's good company.   Very good company. Beer, wine. Or wine, beer. Good conversation. And more.'

'When I go to the Crown, frankly, it's to get a break. Karen always knew how to talk. Yes. But she didn't know when to stop. Of course things change over time.'

'So why were you together then?'

'Crap! That's tight. Hand me a No 6 – No the other one. Ta.'

'Well?'

'Well what?'

'So what is it between you and Karen these days?'

'Habit mate. Just habit.'

'Is that all?'

'Listen, Martin, I don't like bloody talking about it, ok?'

'Well, yes sir! Stiff upper lip, eh Bob?'

'Martin, do you want a No 6 through your head or can I get on with this bloody job?'

'You can get on with the job. And I offered to help, remember?'

'Well just shut up and let me think. The bloody wood is rotten right through. No good just painting over it! It's on its last legs.'

'New frames?'

'Nah! That would cost a fortune...So anyway where does this racy chic of yours hang out?'

'She's not a chick! She'd ring your scraggy neck, Bob, if she heard you say that. She's a very beautiful woman.'

'Oh gawd. Don't tell me you're in luv!'

'Well yes, why not?'

'Won't last mate, wait till the bills start coming in!'

'What bills?'

'Oh there are a lot of bills. So what does this Teressa do, then, to make a buck?'

'FK Franchise if you must know. Classy accessories. Fairtrade'

'Martin? That sounds like swearing, mate.'

'I swear to God!'

'FKFranchising? So does that mean Fucking Franchising? Well, I should get out more, obviously. Is she a bit of a looker, then?'

'She is but she's a lot more than that. Bloody men! What creeps we are! We're mates! Bob, don't you want to know anything about her?'

'Ah shit. OK, Martin, tell me your glorious love story about Teressa.'

'Well, not with that attitude.'

'Oh so sorry. Give me a No 4 then, and tell me all about it in your own time. OK?'

'You're such a stereotype Bob. You're a self-parody man! It's just like a bad script played over and over.'

'Look, Martin. I have my feelings and I keep them under wraps, OK? That's how I deal with it. So, as far as I get it: this new chic of yours has a big red car, wears jewellery, and lives near some bells. That's not exactly an in-depth profile of your new squeeze is it?'

'Well, if you shut your trap a bit more, Bob, you might learn something.'

'La, la, la...'

'Anyway, so far it's going really well.'

'Honeymoon phase like?'

'More than that, much more than that.'

'You never can tell, Bob, what's round the corner. Things can change very quickly.'

'You never know if you don't start.'

'OK Martin, fair dos. Just don't give her the keys too soon, OK? That's my advice.'

'Thank you for your kind advice, Bob.'

'That sounds like you're not taking my advice. Anyway, it's getting dark. Hand me a No 7. We'll need to pack in soon.'

'Yeah, fancy a pint at the Crown?'

'Now you're talking sense!'

'That's what I feared.'

'Serious though, glad it's going well mate. Keep talking but watch out for expensive habits. That's what I say. And I hope it lasts. You never know what's round the corner.'

'Yeah, yeah. Well, anyway, Bob you'll probably make more sense when you're   drunk.'

'Yeah, that's what I say! That's why I do it, Martin. It's my little secret.'

'Well, we're spending Christmas together. And seeing her friends, my friends. Doing   things we both like. It's still developing. We talk, we share stuff, it feels good. Special. Very special.'

'Now mate, the mention of 'special' makes me think of lager.'

'Well, Bob, put the wrench away, have a piss, and get out of your overalls.'

'OK, I concede Round 1. You're lucky mate. Very lucky. Let's go down to the Crown and have a toast to your Terresa.'

'First sensible thing you've said all afternoon.'

'Bloody lucky, you are, bloody lucky.'

'Bloody lucky we are. Well, Teressa and me, I mean.'

'Cheers!'

'Cheers!'

'I can't do without a pint of this every day. That's my medicine.'

'So, Bob, tell me, do you still keep up with Karen a bit?'

'Of course, I've bloody visited her every day for months!'

'Bob! That's a lot of contact for an ex. Does it work?'

'I admit, Martin, it's been difficult. At the care home, I mean. You see, since Karen had the stroke last year, she doesn't even know who the fuck I am.'

Mike Harmer *started writing stories before he was a teenager but this obsession was never diagnosed. Mrs Mainprize, his English teacher, encouraged the class*   *(PTO)* *to write and write, to look around and write some more. His mother always put writing before house work. Mike followed the path of these inspirational women: scribbling from London to Bangor, Marburg to Morelia, Nairobi to Havana. In 1982 he accidentally hitchhiked to Brighton. He has since published: articles in academic journals on the voluntary sector; short fiction for Epoch magazine, NightWriters' publications' and over a 100 theatre reviews for Brighton Source. At Open Mic sessions he has sung his lyrics, accompanied by acoustic guitar, to audiences nearly reaching double figures.*

Zichrova Livrocha
(may her memory be a blessing)

by David Benedictus

A blurred snapshot is all we have.
Betty looks to the right of camera
Smiling – as I thought at first –
Or is she terrified?
Her curly hair in big bunches
And her eyes –
Those burning eyes!

She wears a striped blouse
With a turned down collar –
Very smart, Betty –
For a special occasion.
Most likely the only blouse she had,
The only one she has now for sure
And for ever.

She may have come on a train
As many did in '42,
From Slovakia,
From the West.
Seeking security in those bleak huts
(Oh, but it was so cold!)
And bodies everywhere.
The children and women at the front
('We would have had to feed them,'
Said the man in charge at I.G.Farben,
'And if they cannot work they must not eat.

Why pay a child to work? That would be crazy.
Or let her laugh or live?'

There were two cottages in the forest
A couple of miles away.
'I'm too tired to walk, Mama,
And it's so cold.'
'Hush, Betty, there'll be milk there,
And a warm bed.'

There is no milk, and no warm bed.

After they have taken off their clothes –
'This is good, liebling,
They will be bringing us fresh ones
From the laundry.'

The windows are bricked up
And there is a grating sound
As the heavy keys are turned in the lock.
Down the chimney
Like presents from Santa
Come canisters of Zyklon B
Potassium for milk
And no warm bed
And no sweet-scented clothes.
Just the stink of death
Drowned out by the revving engines
Of the motor-bikes.
'Oh, Mama, Mama, what is that nasty smoke
And this smell?
And where is the milk you promised me?'
I wish Betty was alive

For she was younger than I.
And I would give her milk
And maybe some toys
And I would tell her things, try to explain,
And kiss her,
But she would know more than I
She would know everything.
The little girl with her bunches,
And huge, terrified eyes.
She would come to tea,
An old lady now, of course,
And I would turn on the electric fire
In Harpenden, maybe, or St John's Wood.
'No, dear,' she would say, 'just the milk.'

Maybe I would let her know
That I, and many others, saw the photographs,
And the eyes, and the striped blouse,
I would tell her that she was famous now and loved, more than I can say.
She would answer that it was a very long time ago
And that even ghosts feel pain when they think
That maybe
It is happening again.

RIP Betty Benedictus

The Dentists of Hove
by David Benedictus

Hove is for dentists who offer you everything,
Regular, dazzling teeth, of course,
But more, much more, than that;
Reassurance.
Dr Mohamed said to me:
'I like this place;
It's my home now.
Look! There on the piano –
The portraits of my seven children,
      my displaced babies.
Are they not handsome?

In Hove the flowers are brighter
The flags more boisterous
The men more thrusting and evenly tanned
The women, even the matrons,
Leave off their knickers
      to stroll along the front,
Just in case.
The stucco in Hove is creamier, the
      sea-gulls more harmonious.
The Council has seen to this under Any Other Business.
'And there is a God, of course,'
The good Dr Mohamed adds,
'Who holds each one of us in the palm
      of His hand
Like nesting birds.

Have a rinse now, please.'

The tsunami has arrived
by Enzo Marra

The tsunami has arrived

I try to keep my distance

The tsunami has arrived

I try to evade its advances

The tsunami has arrived

I refuse to reply in kind

The tsunami has peaked

I find crevice to hibernate

The tsunami has peaked

I out of body observe

The tsunami has passed

I am temperate woken

The tsunami has passed

I open eyes in kinder light

The tsunami has passed

I keep my windows battened

Little miracles
by Enzo Marra

Little miracles

how I found you

how we grew together

how we besotted love

how we quarrel hurt

how we always forgave

how we span decades

how we still wobble

how we get back up

how tomorrow is brighter shared

how thankful we are

for little miracles

Enzo Marra *is a painter and poet based in London.*

He has been previously published by the Shadow Archer Press and the Tangerine Press.

Letter to You
by Libby Proe

The knot of hair bounces on the top of your head when you stand. As you raise your arms above your head the tight sleeveless gun-metal grey top moves up towards your waist. Your brow is glistening, after a few moments, you bend down keeping your legs almost straight. Keep practising you will get them straight soon. The bright blue material of your leggings stretches where you bend. Only the tops of your thighs and your lower back are visible.

You stand bringing your hands palm to palm above your head, then lower them down to rest your thumbs on your chest, close your eyes and bow your head.

Once you finish you reach to the side and come back with a glass of water. It is one of your everyday glasses, not the ones you offer to guests. It must have been on the small glass coffee table that is in front of your navy sofa.

You spot a small robin on the windowsill. You move closer, sipping your water. You stare as the bird hops to the end of the sill. It stops right in front of you and tilts its head to the left. A car door slams, the robin spreads its wings and takes flight back to its nest in the hollow of the tree in your garden. You step away from the window and out of sight.

*****

You leave the house giving the door a good pull and push to check that the Yale lock is secure. Only then do the keys materialise.

You put the key into the lock and turn it anti-clockwise to secure the deadlock. It is the same routine every time.

You are wearing that top. You know the one. The old favourite which has seen better days. It has a hole in one of the seams at the left armpit, which you think no one notices. They do.

Heading towards work you take the same route as usual. Even though it takes a little longer you walk along the greener streets rather than the quicker treeless ones. Your pace slows as you turn your head. It is lovely at the moment as the trees are just starting to blossom. As you walk under one of them, some of the pollen falls onto your right shoulder.

You do not notice.

It is Thursday, time for your well-deserved end-of-the-week extravagance. You go into the coffee shop for your customary treat, a large latte with a sprinkle of cinnamon and a blueberry muffin with crystallised sugar on top. It is naughty, and you know it. It is wrong, but that doesn't stop you. After all, you did yoga this morning. You add sugar to the coffee stirring it clockwise 1, 2, 3, 4, 5, 6 times, that's one more than usual. You put the coffee up to your nose before you take a sip. Just a small sip to check that it is right. The latte has given you a white foamy moustache. You wipe it away with the back of your hand. How unseemly. What would your mother say?

You turn your head left and right to look around. Is there someone watching you?

*****

You arrive at work, sit at your desk you go through the post on your desk. You open the letter with a brown envelope, look over the contents and then place the white paper in your intray and throw the envelope away. What no recycling? That is when you find the letter. It looks different from the others. It is not the usual office mail. It is in a blue envelope and with a stamp of a painting of a gymnast from the 2012 Olympics. She is wearing the red, white and blue team leotard, her leg is bent up behind her, the artist has captured the tensions in the muscles she is using for the manoeuvre. You have no choice you open that letter leaving the others on the desk. Leaning back in the chair you open the envelope. The smell of cinnamon reached your nose. You take the letter out, it is on matching blue paper. You read through the letter. Your eyes scan over the words again and again. You open the envelope wider and find the photograph. Hold it gently in your hand. Scrutinising it. Your forehead furrows - you like what you see, your nostrils flare your mouth twitches – to anyone else looking, your face gives none of the joy away. You turn a vivid red. You rip the photograph into tiny pieces. Good idea, you do not want anyone else to see it. It is just for you.

    You sit for a few moments motionless. You pick the letter back up and read the contents again. Then you pick up the phone and call someone. As you speak to them you brush the hair away from your face, your lips move quickly. You move the phone from one hand to the other so you can tap your index finger on the desk. You pick up a pen and begin to write on a pile of bright pink sticky notes on your desk. it is not a happy conversation. Who is the person who has made you so upset? You stand and pace your office, waving your free hand forcefully in front of you. The motion of your arm causes the pollen to fall off your right shoulder. The phone call is not very long – 2 minutes maximum. When you hang up the phone you are out of breath. You pick up the letter again read through it once more then place it and the pieces of the photograph back in the envelope and quickly put it all in the drawer. The monitor rocks on your desk. Probably best to put it away so no one else will see.

    You go to the window and taking the loop of cord to your right in both hands, you pull it putting one hand over the other, closing the blinds. Shutting yourself away from prying eyes.

Expansion
by Leila Bendimered

Life only has one destination: death.

And sometimes, it's good to be reminded of that fact.

I've stopped looking for the key to happiness, love or fulfilment,

Because these are simply not doors.

Just like unhappiness, loneliness or failure,

States of mind are only temporary.

It would be futile to try to capture them,

Or run away from them at all costs.

The only journey that I am called to go on in this lifetime is one of expansion.

And someone I will never know once said that:

"Suffering is the fastest path to awaken consciousness".

It took me a long time to embody this age-old wisdom,

And learn how to waltz with my oldest demons.

The very ones I had tried to hide with all the truths that

this world does not want to hear.

How difficult it is to look at oneself in the mirror,

The rotten wounds are just too ugly.

Once this crucial step has been taken,

I must learn to listen.

Not to other people of course,

They don't know anything about my deepest desires.

Nor do they know about theirs, unfortunately.

Silencing the outside world, but also the hubbub that drums inside my being.

All these voices that contradict each other endlessly.

Shut up!

It's when the silence finally settles that I can hear their song.

I take the hand of the lost child who had been waiting for me for so long.

Together, we go on a desire hunt,

Ignoring all the imaginary obstacles that never really stood in our way.

She teaches me to blindly follow the voice of intuition,

And trust the thousand coincidences and synchronicities that seem to drive my very existence.

I let myself be swept away by the current of life without opposing the slightest resistance,

Since it will inevitably carry me to its one and only destination.

And I Stood
by Debbie Waldon

I stood, I waited and I watched for you.

The tears that wouldn't come before came now.

I recalled the way you looked when you looked at me.

I recalled the words you spoke when you spoke to me.

And though you cannot hear me, I speak to you now.

And though you cannot see me, I see you now.

See you as you were before,

remember you before the day that was to be the last of days

for you forever more.

And my tears flowed from my eyes and overflowed my lashes,

fell from my face and would not stop.

The tears flowed to cover me and where I had walked,

they covered the sod and glistened in the sun.

I stood beneath the trees and I became a tree.

I stood where no one could see, and the tears became a river

and the river was made of me and made of my love for you.

And the river dried and stayed in the woods where I wait for you.

I stood, I waited and I watched for you. But you did not come.

Houses
by Debbie Waldon

You shot me. Two bullets left your gun. One hit. That's all it took, a single bullet working alone speeding its way through my eye, muscle, brain, skull. My blood running crimson into my ear, down my neck, dripping from my chin, staining my white blouse, white bra, creating a kaleidoscopic pattern on the orange wall. Red, orange, red, orange.

I watched you as you put the gun down on the table by the window of the derelict house you'd lured me to. Watched you gaze out at the cityscape skyline and further up to the peaceful blue sky. Watched you open the window and take in a few deep cleansing breaths. Then you left, discarding your gloves in a bin halfway to your office as you saw the dustcart moving slowly towards it.

Weeks later you came to my funeral; your eyes leaked tears. Who were the tears for? For me? For you? For show?

You threw a posy of wild flowers, my favourite, on top of my coffin as it was lowered into the ground. You put your arm around my mother's shoulder, rested your head on hers, shared a packet of tissues. Together you walked to the cemetery gates and into the waiting car.

You were at her side day after day offering comfort, sharing grief and memories, working your way into her affections, proving your 'love' for me. No one would suspect otherwise. You listened to all that the police had to say on my murder, their investigation, lack of clues, lack of suspects.

You had a water-tight alibi; you'd been at the office all day. Your secretary, who you'd been sleeping with for the past six years, confirmed, as you'd asked her to, that you'd not left your office all day; that she'd brought a sandwich to your desk.

My will stated that with all my worldly goods I thee endowed.

In my home, left to me by my father, you tore down walls, re-built the kitchen, changing cosy Victoriana into modern minimalism. You watched property programmes to see how to make a fast buck out of your inheritance.

Late one night you came downstairs unable to sleep. In the glow of the halogen lights, you could see a kaleidoscopic pattern on the wall. Red and orange on the white wall. You went back to bed but couldn't sleep.

In the morning you got into the car and drove to my mother's house to take her to the cemetery. Tears once more flowed from both of you, from her they were felt, and watered the cherry tree you planted together there in my name. You thought it would be a nice touch.

When we had first moved in to my house together you'd

carved our initials inside a heart onto a cherry tree in the garden, planted by my father on the day I was born. After my death it was the first thing you had ripped up by the landscape gardener.

Back at home you noticed blood dripping from the taps. Drip, drip, drip. In the morning you shouted at the plumber; demanded that the builders work faster, harder.

That night you saw my face in the pizza delivered to your door. The first white hairs showed at your temples, though you weren't aware of them.

At work the lack of sleep was causing you to make mistakes. Your manner was no longer mild. You were ordered to take sick leave. Grief does terrible things to a person.

Your secretary told you she could no longer put up with you. She didn't understand; you'd never loved your wife, only married her for her money. She'd never tell, of course; her brother's revolver was the one you left on the table in the room where I died.

When you got home my wedding ring, which you'd last seen on my finger in the open coffin, was now on the coffee table on top of the book of modern art that I'd bought for you for Christmas that you'd given to a charity shop.

Your doctor gave you the drugs you needed to sleep. In

your dreams I comforted you with my skeleton hands.

You went away for a period of rest into a nice house in the country with doctors and nurses and more drugs. The health insurance I took out on you paid for your stay there. In the night you screamed and had to be sedated.

In the mornings your personal belongings weren't where you'd left them. Other people's belongings had found their way into your room. You swore that you never stole. During the day you rocked to and fro. You saw things that other people didn't see and heard things other people didn't hear.

Months later my mother moved into the house that I inherited from my father, that you inherited from me, that your conscience, what little you had left, persuaded you to give to her in the hope it would provide you with the peace you craved. Your modernisations made it easier for her to get around in her wheelchair.

The insurance used to pay for your care didn't last and now you look out of the windows of a different house, a drab, grey house on the edge of town. The windows of the house have bars; the doors of the house have locks. It is a house you'll never leave.

Nor There
by Mark Burrow

Dreaming about mum. Walking along a country lane. We saw plump birds appear from the tall grass and scuttle across the road. They had brown feathers, speckled black, and jade green necks. I asked mum why they didn't fly.

They're pheasants, she said. You eat them.

I didn't want to chew on the flesh of a living creature. That felt like a cruel and senseless thing to do. The birds hopped onto the berm of sun-bleached grass and then into the gloom of a wood filled with long thin pine trees. Sweat dripped down my forehead and into my eyes, making them sting. We kept on walking along the lane. It was a hot afternoon and I was thirsty. There was the sound of crickets chirping in the grass. They got louder and I wanted to cover my ears. Except I had to wee and was using a hand to squeeze my crotch.

Stop playing with yourself, mum said.

I needed to go. I was busting. I knew that if I weed against a pine tree then a terrible thing would happen. Mum walked faster than me. I couldn't keep up. We passed a thatched cottage and there was smoke curling out of a chimney. I wondered why someone was burning a wood fire on a blistering summer's day. I asked mum if we could stop by the cottage and use their toilet. She didn't hear me because of the noise of the crickets.

A gust of warm wind blew along the lane, stirring up clouds of dust. I walked as quickly as I could, squeezing myself, trying to hold in the pee, feeling my bladder about to burst. Mum didn't turn around. She stared ahead, walking straight, handbag hanging off her shoulder. The crickets were loud. I didn't know where we were heading. I couldn't turn around. I was clueless as to where we had come from.

I was grateful for the breeze. I wondered if I should stop and wee at the side of the lane. Mum wasn't looking over her shoulder. I started to hear an engine mixed in with the crickets and saw a blue tractor crossing a field, heading towards us, towing a wheeled metal contraption. I called out to mum. I asked her to wait for me. The tractor was noisier than the crickets. It was getting closer by the second. Rolling towards us. I had to wee. I felt a squirt come out and wet my pants. I didn't know what to do. I looked at the tractor and saw water spray out of the thin bars it was pulling across the grass. I thought that the farmer must be watering the field. He was driving quickly and came parallel to the barbed wire fence that separated his field from the narrow lane. I looked at the cabin and saw a man with scars on his face. I called out to mum. She couldn't hear me. The water from the rattling bars started to spray over me and I caught a sickening turd-filled whiff that made me gag. The liquid was some kind of fertilizer. I started to retch at the smell, covering my eyes and mouth, crying out to mum, feeling the release and shame of warm wee soaking through my jeans and trickling down my legs.

***

I wake up and it's dark.

I'm on the top bunk in my cell.

I've wet myself in my sleep again. I have this trippy, confused sense of still feeling as if I'm in my dream, like my brain is stretched over different times and places. I slip off my pants, balling them under the pillow. I pat the sheets and there's a small patch of dampness. Gradually feeling more together and with it, I sit up and realise there is still an awful turdy stink in the cell. I notice a small light in the corner and a humming sound. It's Tom, my cellmate. I whisper his name. I pull on a pair of joggers and jump off the top bunk, trying not to breathe in. I see that he's reaching into the toilet and then smearing what he's pulled out of the water onto the wall.

I gag twice and say, "Tom, what are you playing at?"

He pats the wall.

"Tom."

"Painting," he says.

"Do what?"

"This place needs a lick of paint."

He pulls a fresh lump out of the toilet water, humming merrily to himself.

I push the buzzer for the Guard.

Tom doesn't pay any attention. I stand in the corner and

hold a pillow against my face to stifle the smell. He killed his step-father with a letter opener after being told he couldn't go to Thorpe Park with his mates. The Guard eventually arrives and unlocks the door. I'm ordered to stand in the corridor and wait. Tom flicks and chucks turds at the Guard and smears whatever he can in brown until more arrive. They get hold of him and give him a proper kicking.

It wakes up the other lads. As per usual, the cell warriors bawl, holler and jeer at the Guards.

I'm taken to a different block and put in a room with a kettle, tea bags and UHT milk, so I make a cuppa and stand by the window, watching the black night fade from the sky as the sun rises. I hope the Guards don't find my wet underpants tucked beneath my pillow. I don't know why I keep wetting the bed. I think it might be the tablets they've put me on for my moods.

I sip the tea and think about how life's a joke. Tom decorating his cell. Me – nearly beating a stranger in a pin-stripe suit to death for jumping the queue at the bus stop outside college.

Alarms will be going off in towns and cities across the country, waking up normal people to go about their mundane lives.

I wonder about mum. She liked to have a lie-in. I remember that about her before she left.

I'm not a morning person, she used to say.

I guess she's asleep in a warm cosy bed, living with a rich bloke in a house in the country.

I doubt I ever live in her dreams like she lives in mine.

The Grizzling
by Mark Burrow

Anne scrunched a wet flannel and pressed it against my eye. The coldness made me flinch.

"Keep still," she said, acting like she was my mum. "Now you hold the flannel."

I did as I was told, sitting on the side of the bath, hearing her open the cupboard under the sink, searching for a bottle of antiseptic.

"It stinks of rats in here."

Anne talked a lot about rats that summer. Looking back now, I can remember how everyone on the estate was obsessed. The dustmen were on strike and the rubbish kept piling higher, creating these pyramids of plastic bags that brought out a plague of vermin.

"This will sting."

The liquid sloshed against the glass of the bottle and then she pushed a wet ball of cotton wool against the graze on my left leg.

"Are you going to tell me who did this to you?"

I passed her the flannel and she soaked it under the tap. She dried her hands on a small towel and poured more stingy stuff onto the cotton. "Who did this?"

"Bobby."

"Bobby who?"

"Lives in the flats over the road."

"Well, it's got to stop."

She could've asked more questions. I was grateful she didn't.

I sensed Anne didn't really care about me. My real mum left when I was a few years younger. She promised to come back and take me with her. We talked on the landline phone and she named the day and time she was coming. Dad helped me pack a suitcase. I was allowed to take one big toy and a few tiny ones. I stood on the balcony of the flats, waiting for a blue car to arrive, driven by a man I didn't know. I went downstairs and stood by a bollard, holding my suitcase, as if standing nearer to the road would make them come faster. My heart pumped like mad when I saw a blue car turn into the estate. I started waving and then realised the car was driving straight by. I can still see the face of an old lady with thick glasses, staring at me through the passenger window.

Dad appeared and touched me on the shoulder. 'She's not coming, son. I can't get her on the phone.'

We walked back to the stairwell in the block of flats. 'I'm afraid you're stuck with me.'

The locks on my suitcase popped open and my toys fell out with my clothes. To me, they resembled a jumble of broken promises.

Dad told me to see the funny side. 'If you don't laugh, you'll cry.'

I noticed how he wasn't laughing.

***

Anne said I had to take dad to the flat where Bobby lived. I was on dad's side, saying we shouldn't go. Anne didn't listen. I said dad's right and they both told me to stay out of it.

As per usual, dad lost the row.

I slipped into my fake Adidas. They had two stripes instead of three. Dad laced up his work boots.

"This can't go on," said Anne.

I wasn't sure if she was talking about me or something else.

I traipsed behind dad on the balcony. He walked with his hands in his pockets, slouched and muttering to himself. When we reached the stairwell, he swivelled round and said, "Don't tell your mum, but I've been laid off."

What he was saying went over my head. I wanted to say to him that Anne wasn't my mum but I had the nous to keep that thought to myself. We walked down the concrete stairs. The air on the ground floor, with high-rises all around us, smelled of rotten food. Me and dad were used to the stink by then. We passed the pile of bags where Bobby punched me.

"Look at the size of that bugger," said dad, pointing to a rat.

We entered a block of flats and walked up the stairwell to

the third floor, not bothering with a lift because they never worked. Bobby's mum sat in the doorway on a deck chair. She wore a pink cotton smock and had long, greasy brown hair. There was a tattoo of a dagger stabbing a heart on her right arm. She sucked on a Coke flavoured jubbly and fanned herself with cardboard ripped off a cereal box. Dad started talking. I seriously didn't want to be there, so I looked out towards the flats and the tower block. The sun was setting and it turned the windows and bricks the colour of orangeade.

"I want to have a word with you about my lad."

"What's he got to do with me?"

"Check out the state of his face."

I was made to turn round.

The mum smirked.

"All I'm asking is for your boy not to smack him around."

"Boy?"

"It's not on.

She crunched her jubbly and shouted with a mouthful of broken ice, "Bobby, get down here."

A girl's voice came from inside the flat, hollering, "What for?"

"Get here," shouted the mum.

Dad was confused. He tapped me on the arm.

Bobby appeared in the doorway. She was short, chubby and a girl. "What's he doing here?" she said and then, looking directly at me, she added, "Get away or do you want more licks?"

The mum raised her hand to stop her mouthing off. "Tell them what he did."

"What for?"

"Because I'm telling you to."

Bobby folded her arms and said, "He was running around with a rat stuck on the end of a stick. It was disgusting. The stick went through the rat's mouth and eyeball. So, I tells him to stop and he goes and shoves this rat-stick close to my mouth and then says my knickers smell like the rubbish tip so I take the stick off-of him and give him proper licks."

The mum nodded with approval.

We didn't have a leg to stand on. We should have walked off, heads bowed, so I don't know what came over dad.

"That's your attitude, is it?" he said. "Two wrongs make a right? You call that parenting?"

The mum handed the jubbly to Bobby and dropped her Coco Pops fan. "Do what?"

"You heard."

"She was sticking up for herself."

"She went too far."

"Teach your boy to stand up for himself and he won't get

hit by a girl."

"Don't tell me how to raise my kid."

"But you'll stand there telling me how to raise mine?"

I tug dad's t-shirt.

Bobby chipped in, "That's right, you better go, you weedy grizzling."

Dad snapped at her, "Shut your mouth."

I felt the mood change right there.

Bobby's mum pushed herself up. The deck chair wobbled under her weight. She wiped her sticky hands on her smock and then punched dad on the nose. I fell backwards as dad staggered against me. She charged him and he regained his balance and threw a right hook that caught her on the ear. They both dropped to the floor and wrestled. She sank her teeth into his arm, making him scream. He yanked her hair and then kneed her hard in the fanny. A Rasta, who lived next door, rushed out and forced them apart. Dad's nose was dripping blood. I took off my t-shirt and handed it to him. The shoulder of Bobby's mum's smock was torn and her greyish bra was showing. I pulled dad away, hearing the mum and Bobby yelling abuse at us. We only stopped when we were in the stairwell, away from the other tenants who had stepped out of their council flats onto their balconies to see where the screaming and hollering was coming from. Dad breathed heavily. He checked the bitemark on his forearm and pulled out his pack of ciggies from his jeans, finding one that wasn't broken. He lit a fag, tilting his head back and wiping blood with my t-shirt.

"Dad, I know I should have told you Bobby's a girl."

"It's alright," he said.

"I'm sorry."

"It's fine, son," he said. "Everything's going to be alright."

***

We walked across the estate. Rats scuttled close to the walls. I wondered what they dreamed about when sleeping. Fields of rubbish and carcasses stretching to the horizon. Maybe the estate was a kind of paradise for rodents. We walked up the stairwell. When we arrived at our front door, which was the same colour as all the rest, dad played pat-a-cake with his pockets. "Do you have a key?"

"Nope."

He tossed his fag over the balcony and tried to flick the letterbox. The flap hardly budged as the spring was too tight. He banged on the door's wired glass with a fist.

Anne answered. Dad was holding my t-shirt against his busted nose, blood splattered down his front. I was bare-chested and covered in more cuts and grazes.

"You've got to be kidding?"

I followed dad in. Anne went off on one. She accused me and dad of all sorts. Saying we made her life a misery.

Dad said he told her it was a mistake to go over.

I wondered if I should have 'fessed up from the start about

running around with a rat on a stick. It was supposed to be funny. All the other kids were laughing. I really believed it wasn't my fault Bobby couldn't take a joke.

Anne locked herself in the bedroom. Dad went to the bathroom and sat on the side of the bath. I soaked a flannel under the cold tap and handed it to him so he could wipe the blood. I removed balls of cotton wool from the pack in the smelly cupboard under the sink. He pushed them into his nostrils and asked for the bottle of antiseptic, wetting a piece of wool and dabbing the bite.

We could hear Anne crying, saying it was over between her and dad.

He touched my shoulder, trying to make me feel better. "It's not your fault," he said, smiling, except his smile didn't match the worry in his eyes. It reminded me of how he looked in the days after mum left.

Some people, they go and never come back.

Small Town Insurrection
by Mark Burrow

I walked through the maze of streets and alleyways, trying to remember how to reach the town square. Seagulls circled above me, swooping low overheard and crying out like I was a scrap of food to be snaffled in their beaks.

A swarm of grey clouds filled the evening sky. There was nobody around to ask for directions. Somewhere far off, I heard the barking of a black dog. The noise made me feel wistful. I looked at the curtains pulled shut across the windows of cobblestone cottages and slanted, two-up, two-down houses. I sensed that the entire town was on the cusp of an immense tragedy. The citizens were going to be gripped by violent urges, refusing to cower in their homes any longer, arming themselves with carving knives, cricket bats, rolling pins and homemade petrol bombs.

In a fearsome mob, they would break into cars, shy stones at windows, tip over rubbish bins and set them ablaze. Their fury was directed at the Mayor, the Chief of Police, the President of the Rotary Club, the Leader of the Book Club, former car insurance CEOs and the highest echelons of Government. The people couldn't feed and clothe themselves, let alone their families. They wanted real jobs, affordable homes, decent education, and to be able to take their children to X-on-Sea's beach without them getting sick from the sewage and filth in the sea due to the shady dealmaking and backhanders of the corrupt executives at the water company.

The people were cynical about the grand Art Exposition and what it would do to the town, effectively making it a theme park for wannabe artists and hangers-on, unsavoury individuals who were infamous for their loose morals, alcoholism, drug-taking, scrounging and slovenly work ethic. The deranged citizens would rampage through the streets, beating their chests, bearing their arses, grabbing their crotches and smacking their hands against their mouths and whooping like Apache warriors used to do in politically incorrect cowboy movies, heading in an angry hoard ever closer to the mythical town square.

As the scenes of carnage unfolded, desperate calls would be made by the Mayor, Chief of Police and the heads of the Rotary and Book Clubs.

"We have to do something," cried the President of the Rotary Club, a man with a moustache who was proud of his golf handicap and pilot's licence.

"Call the police," exclaimed the Leader of the Book Club, a woman who was obsessed with the poetry of Alfred Tennyson.

"You call the police," he said.

"Why me?" she replied.

"You know why."

There was a rumour that the Leader of the Book Club was in a long-standing affair with the Chief of Police.

As the two of them argued, the Mayor was frantically calling the Chief of Police, who was out on his yacht, *Lucky Pierre*. He was with his wife and two teenage sons, feeling resentful as he wanted to be with the Leader of the Book Club as he regarded her as his first and truest love.

"It's my day off," said the Chief of Police.

"Rome is burning," yelled the Mayor.

"Are you calling me *Nero*?"

"Did I say you're Nero?"

"What's Rome burning got to do with me?"

They disliked each other intensely. Both thought the other was an out an out narcissist and unfit for their roles of office.

"The riots," shouted the Mayor.

The Chief of Police sighed, looking at his wife on a sun lounger, sipping a glass of chardonnay and reading a fashion magazine, wondering how much he would lose if he tried to divorce her.

"And what part of, 'It's-my-day-off', do you not comprehend'?"

The Mayor wanted to smash the phone against a wall. "What are you talking about? The part where there is a riot and there won't be a town to police if you don't so something. Stop dilly-dallying on Lucky Pierre – Rome is burning."

"So, you *are* calling me Nero?" said the Chief of Police, who was smarting because of the budget cuts the Mayor had made, forcing him to reduce the number of police he had to keep the town safe. It was delusional to think he had the resources to stop the burglaries and spate of dog snatching, let alone a full scale riot. Not that the Chief of Police was going to demean himself by bringing up that thorny issue again. He wanted to know why the Mayor was calling him a crazed Roman Emperor. "If anyone is Nero in this town, it's you."

They stayed on the phone, arguing about ancient Romans with serious mental health issues.

The Leader of the Book Club didn't think it was her place to call the police. "I'm not doing it and that's final," she said to the President of the Rotary Club, who she thought was a poser, calling him a big mouth behind his back. "Goodbye," she said, hanging up the phone. The Chief of Police was the last person she wanted to speak to, especially when he was out sailing with his family on their yacht. She was doing her utmost not to think about him and what might have been if the two of them had got together and had sons of their own. The sorrow welled up inside of her at the thought she had squandered her life in the hope that he would keep his promise of leaving his wife. It was never going to happen and she was semi-resigned to living by herself, working during the day for the local Council, processing welfare claims, knowing that her colleagues referred to her behind her back as a "dried fruit", and spending her evenings with a radio on low for the comfort of background noise, her head buried in books of rhyme.

When she put the phone down, she heard the whoops of rioters charging through her street. Taking a pocket torch from a drawer in her bedside cabinet, where she kept it due to an increase in power cuts, she crawled under her single bed and tried to pacify the fears in her brain and her heart by reading about Arthurian legend.

***

In the charred and smoky aftermath of the riot, the media would focus heavily on the untimely and grisly demise of the President of the Rotary Club, who had made his fortune after taking over his father's shop, 'The Fudge Pantry', and growing it into a national franchise. A confirmed bachelor with a reputation for being a playboy, he had been thinking of emigrating anyway, wanting to spend his retirement by a pool, baking under the heat of the Mediterranean sun, ideally in a country that wasn't "too foreign", where he could have a Full English breakfast at least a couple of days a week, play a round of golf on a decent course, and watch the matches of his favourite rugby team in a bar. He was convinced that the rioters had grown into an unstoppable tsunami of hate, that they had been consumed by the type of bloodlust and madness that can only occur in crowds. He put on his brown leather jacket, motorcycle helmet and goggles, kick-starting his Triumph TR6.

As he sped to the local airport where he kept his airplane, he didn't see the fishing wire that two fishermen had pulled across the road. They had wrapped the wire around sycamore trees on either side and pulled it tight by tying perfect knots, making it precisely neck height for the President of the Rotary Club. The fishermen, hiding behind bushes, gave each other a high five as they heard the rumbling engine of the motorbike, remembering how the President of the Rotary Club had told them, when drunk on expensive whiskey in the pub, that "tourists couldn't give a toss about fishing anymore". They watched him on the bike, angling round a bend, going way over the speed limit as per usual, and then turning onto a straight stretch of road and pulling the brakes at the last second after seeing a glint of sunlight on the wire. They briefly feared he might skid underneath and were relieved to see that he was too late – the wire cut neatly into his neck, slicing his head clean off.

The fishermen watched the sight of his head flying through the air like a football and, ever so briefly, his body staying on the seat of the bike, hands on the handlebars, resembling a phantom headless motorcycle rider in a leather jacket on a ghost journey to haunt the airport. Normality resumed when blood fountained from his neck, the body limply tumbled onto the road, and the bike careered into a tree and exploded. They jumped to their feet and did a second high-five, satisfied by a job well done, hurrying to re-join the rioters to maintain a cover story of sorts for when the police investigated who was responsible for the decapitation, so they could say they had been in town rioting all along. The two fishermen agreed it was better to be prosecuted for civil disobedience and public disorder than for murdering the President of the Rotary Club.

I sensed all of this brewing on my walk through the town. Feeling it in the bricks and the mortar of the slanted houses, in the pinks, blues and greens of the facades. It was in the seashell doorbells and the intricate latticework of the wooden porches.

I knew my art would be what brought an end to the riots.

When the mob reached the town square, they would be in a frenzy. Some were intent on building a guillotine, others were content with no-nonsense lynching. The men and women wanted revenge and payback for the years of exploitation, corruption and neglect. The people were furious at how out of touch the Mayor and his cronies were, how oblivious they were to what it was like for ordinary folk to live in X-on-Sea, how tough it was to get by, and how bleak and depressing it was to bring children into a world without any prospects, with no chance of them ever having a synchronised future.

That's when I would appear, walking onto the stage in the

centre of the square, carrying my easel wrapped in velvet cloth with gold embroidery. They would be whooping in my face, making obscene gestures, spitting and scowling, telling me that I was the Mayor's stooge and errand boy. I would keep walking, calm and steady, opening my easel and then raising my hands for them to hush. When they had finally quietened to a level I deemed reasonable, I would remove the velvet cloth and allow them to see my painting of a scotch egg, rendered in the style not of a New Wave Pre-Raphaelite, but a Pointillist.

I'd pick up my easel and slowly rotate, giving every rioter the chance to marvel at my work.

And marvel they would – the crackle of violence falling away from their curled mouths.

Involuntarily, they would cry out, "It's beautiful" and, "Oh, my goodness."

The square would be filled with a perfumed mushroom cloud of love and kindness.

"Are you not astonished?" I would say.

"Yes, we are," they would reply in unison, their voices soft and gooey, like when they spoke to puppies, kittens and newborn babies.

I'd collapse onto the ground, exhausted and drained from my artistic labours and the intensity of my vision. They would take me in and give me a bed, putting a damp cloth on my forehead, tending to me night and day, feeding me homemade broth.

"You're one of us now," a woman would say to me, dipping a flannel in cold water and then placing it on me to cool my fever. "This is where you belong."

"Where am I?" I'd say, delirious.

"Home, my lovely. You're home."

Mark Burrow *has published a novella, Coo, which is about an alcoholic turning into a pigeon in a world where people are turning into birds (Alien Buddha Press). His short stories have appeared in a range of titles, such as Bubble, Literally Stories, Cerasus, Flight of the Dragonfly, Punk Noir Press and Hunger, an anthology of stories published by Urban Pigs Press. He has finished the first draft of a second novel, which needs a long edit. He lives in Brighton in the UK and can be found on social @markburrow20*

Not Weird
by Niall Drennan

He said

Me I don't love cats

Or dogs

I don't mind 'em, though

Same with people

An' some people, well they're more than fine

I'm a person

Or, I think I am

See with cats and dogs…

I don't love 'em
I couldn't sleep with 'em
Or, clean up after them
But I wouldn't keep them hostage in a house

I don't like how all the big cats and lions and zebras an' elephants are in the zoo…

An all those cows an' pigs and sheep and little baby lambs we see roaming the countryside well, I mean I like 'em

But I'm not weird

I wouldn't eat 'em or anything

Let them amble and be who they are

Same as all the other creatures who be different to me

See I can relate to 'em as other creatures

I know they're not ma friends

We be too different for that.

Tarnished Tattoo
by Niall Drennan

I have a tarnished tattoo on my arm that reads,
You are the only one
An' it's still as razor-sharp
As the day I had it done

I have letters tattooed on each finger
To mark our sacred love
It spells the word, 'inseparable'
As in, together, 'hand in glove'

I have a suggestive tattoo
On my prick
It whispers,
'Feel free to bite and nibble'
Once upon a time
there were other words there too
but now they've been reduced to scribble

I have a tattoo on my heart
That I hope instructs my fate
Four letters,
D – N – F – R
Do Not Fuckin' Resuscitate...

Choca
by Niall Drennan

The voice is weak with age,

-What happened to you?

This old man looms as I open my eyes,

- Who the hell are you?

His face sharp and wizened; small sacs of mucus hang from the left enlarged nostril and his blue eyes are wide as he continues to gaze down at me and I say,

-Well?

He seems scared but manages,

-Found you…found you on the bench right here, didn't I?

Wrinkles his nose and gains courage,

-An' you ... an' well…a you look like shit!

I feel like shit but I laugh,

-Well thanks for that

His nostrils twitch as he says,

-Smell like it, too!

I'm about to explain how the kid pelted me with eggs but all I manage is,

-It's not shit ... it's egg ...

He shakes his head,

-Egg? What eat egg, with your head, do you?

This is belligerence,

-No, you stupid old prick. Someone threw eggs at me!

      Through a hazy, swatch of cold, blue light, I watch a younger fellow in a dirty denim jacket and jeans with thin pale strips in the worn knees, rise from his slumber on the grass, stretch out his arms and glance over at me before he say to the older man

-I telt ya to wake me. I'm away now

He moves fast and only then does it occur to me to check my pocket,

-Hey, you, wait a minute

Of course, he's gone and my pocket, previously choca with money, is now empty

-Shit, shit ... shit

When I pull the cut lining of the pocket out; the old man squints,

-What's wrong with you?

I decide to focus on him, rather than the other fellow because there isn't much choice,

-I woke up and I looked up… and I; behold you were there…there over me….looming. How long had you been there?

He studies me with sly intensity,

-Listen, lad, I didn't steal from you!

-Who said you did?

He shakes his head,

-What you looking at me like that for then?

-How do you mean?

-You know, the way you're looking at me now

He has guilt all over him,

-Listen old man, someone has stolen my money

He blinks, and is back fast with,

-Nothing to do with me.

-How did you know about it then?

-It's obvious, I mean ...from the way you're acting!

-Yeah?

He points to a spot, a few metres away,

-I saw some guys talking to you when you were over there, on that bench

This is the first mention of this,

-When?

-Late last night or maybe a few hours ago I don't know ...

His vagueness is believable,

-What happened?

-Three of 'em came over and started talking to you.

-What were they saying?

-I couldn't hear. I was too far away.

He searches his pocket,

-Listen, have you got a ciggie?

I go to a side pocket and find the cut-linings in my jacket,

-You know I haven't got anything, don't you?

He looks down at the ground and spots a discarded

cigarette butt, picks it up and adds it to a small tin,

-Think I'd be doing this, if I 'ad money?

-Means shit. Saying some guys took it, eh? Or, your young friend?

-Maybe they did ... I don't know

I stare at him and bluff,

-It was you? Wasn't it?

He looks down,

-What?

Then he looks up at me with an ugly expression as I say,

-You heard me. Was it you? Were you with them?

-Get ta fu ... I swear. It wasn't me.

-But you were in on it? Their lookout? They gave you money to turn a blind eye?

He shakes his head hard and finally says,

-Not my style, lad.

When he says this, I glimpse another self, a younger man, somewhere in that old, grizzled carcass and I say,

-What do you mean?

He's shaking his head again as he says,

-Rolling drunks for money! Not me.

I wonder if I should believe this,

-I wasn't drunk.

He doesn't care,

-You were off your nut on something

-You live around these parts?

His eyes mist,

-Sometimes. I did once, permanent ... long time back, I used to know a lot of people this way ... you sure you don't have anything to smoke on you?

-Found some on the ground, didn't you?

He looks at me with distaste,

-What about change?

I begin to shake my head, not bothering to speak but it hurts so I say,

-No. Nothing.

His punch surprises me and I fall to my knees

and swear and threaten him,

-You old prick. I'm going to....

I block the kick he aims at my head and I manage to stand up and confront him,

-It was you, wasn't it?

He aims another punch and advances but he's weak and I wait, wait until he is up close, and I hammer my forehead hard into his face.

-Don't ... Help ...

He's on the ground and there is a period of calm until I say,

-All right you piece of shit, where's my money?

I lean over him, listen to his rapid breathing and notice the track marks down his arms,

-Well?

My eyesight is fuzzy and I have a pain from my contact with his bony face

-Cat got your tongue, eh?

There's nothing in his pockets of value and I leave him on the blood stained gravel,

-My guess is your buddy took my money. Well you ole

prick, I hope he spends it all before you can find him.

In Soho Square, a man whistles and yells to those who know,

-I- 'ere now – come ... come. Come peoples ... I 'ere.

His hand is *choca with coins from deals and I move in closer and I ask him,

-What you got? Got something for me?

He shakes his head,

-Sorry

-C'mon, you know I'm good ... an' I'm coming to see you tomorrow, please

There are people behind me as he considers and then relents and soon, a boy with alabaster skin and red hair delivers a bag of heroin to me by bike and later when I see the man again he says,

-The last time. An' make sure you have funds, when I see you tomorrow, right? No more credit!

* Choca:

Definition A: To perform fellatio to the point where the giver throws up from the service. (v).

Perhaps a mixture of 'cock' and 'chuck-up'?

Definition B: Brit-slang for crowded or packed. (adj.)

A contraction for choc-a-block, e.g. 'That road is choca in the mornings.'

Niall Drennan: *I've been involved with NightWriters since I hit on it as a way of staying up late. My Mummy made me hot milk and tucked me up in bed and I'd sneak out and head to my local pub where they had a policy of refusing to serve eight year old children. At the time I was appalled and decided to write about this horrid experience to the current editor of the Times.*

P.S. I am now a staid elderly gentleman of dubious, sartorial taste, once a supporter of the Angry Brigade

https://en.wikipedia.org/wiki/The_Angry_Brigade

Sunnier Days are Not So Far Away
by Marita Wild

Tables on pavements outside public houses
Mums in light blouses and Dads in short trousers
Perfume of lavender and scent of sweet roses
Plump happy babies with cute freckled noses
Sunbeds, striped sunshades, and Singapore Slings
Buckets and spades and Frisbees to fling
Old men on deck chairs sucking in girth
To gaze at bronzed bodies riding the surf
Wives sprawling topless on the seashore
Breasts long as spaniel ears down to the floor
Baby girls toddling in frilly sunbonnets
Eyes full of wonder and smiles like a sonnet
Men playing cricket on emerald green grass
Thwack on the willow and cries of, "Howzat?"
Blankets on sand and glasses of wine
Lips meeting in kisses as bodies entwine
Bracken and ants and unfastened laces
Stinging of nettles in personal places

And then it rained.

Take Heed
by Marita Wild   (with apologies to Jenny Joseph)

When I am old
I will dress in green kaftans
Tuck a rose behind my ear
And wear a purple turban.
I'll sit at pavement cafes in the sun
And drink too much wine
Then laugh when I fall down.

When I am old
I'll travel the world
To Katmandu.
I'll visit Buddhist temples
And ride in brightly coloured rickshaws
I'll trample rice in paddy fields
Laugh and dance with women and girls
In Vietnamese villages

I'll sky-dive from snowy mountains
Learn to water-ski from foreign beaches
Flirt with Italian waiters in Rome
And wink at strange men in the street
  But only the good-looking ones.

Ah but still if I don't get to do any of these things
And when my journey comes to its final end
Then I want each and every person
I met along my way
To know how much I thank you
Especially you my friend
For being my companion
In the dark and in the light.

It was a pleasure to have known you
Who knows if one of us will pass this way again?
And maybe meet once more
And if perchance it should be you
Then look me up knock on my door why don't you
So we can laugh again?

Applications of Artificial Intelligence in Elderly Care Robotics
by Aidan Hopkins

> *The company's better-living platform is a holistic gerontechnology solution that combines the power of AI, 5G, and IoT in health care monitoring and remote consultation. Caregivers looking to improve in-home care quality can leverage the Gravefoot gerontechnology to strengthen connections and create better environments for seniors at home.*
>
>   *Gravefoot.ai website*

"Please return to your bed, Marion!"

It was coming for her down the stairs. She had made it this far but her legs were aching hard now.

She glanced desperately around the strange narrow room. It was kind of domestic and almost familiar, like a house she had once known, but all the doors were gone. The walls were decorated in floral patterns, a large apparently real table held fruit in a bowl. No not just a bowl...this was very weird...her own banana shaped terracotta fruit bowl. She stared at the bowl a micro-second. No, it wasn't hers, of course, but it could almost have been. Think, girl! She was clearly in some sort of food preparing area.

"Please return to your bed, Marion." Shit, it was already whirring electrically down the long hall.

In a panic she cast around for a weapon. Nothing presented itself in the clean environment. Any sort of cooking utensil would do, like a carving knife.

As the thought occurred to her lights flickered across one of the boxy shapes at waist height scattered along the wall to her right. She knew what was going to happen. It had happened before, she realised. Sure enough a translucent panel glowed red and a roast chicken manifested itself jammed in amongst the carcasses of another six in varying states of decay, piled up behind the smoky glass.

An upscaling of the electrical whirr told her that this activity had not passed unnoticed.

"Please return to your bed, Marion."

Door, she thought, frantically. Escape.

Various bars of light flickered on smoothly integrated appliances. Nonsensical symbols manifested themselves, danced and disappeared. No door. It was nearly on her.

Fire! she thought deliberately in a fit of inspiration.

A siren keened terrifically from the ceiling and a light mist began to fall. But, this was not all. Her heart leapt as half a dozen small red canisters manifested themselves in each corner of what she now realised fleetingly was her own kitchen.

"Please return to your bed, Marion." The stubby cylindrical geronto-robot, in friendly pink with an amusing cartoon face and the word "Henry" written across its belly surged in through the accessible doorway, brandishing a syringe.

"Please return to your bed, Marion."

She depressed the trigger and a rush of foam hit the thing where she reckoned its visual sensors were, not its jolly painted eyes. It reacted faster than human speed lunging blindly forward with the needle toward where Marion's legs should have been, but weren't. For she was crouched atop the table and now, with all her strength, brought the ceramic fruit bowl crashing down on the monster's upper surface. The flexiplastic gave but did not crack. Desperately she tried to hoist the heavy bowl for another blow. "Christ" she gasped. A ping told her the oven had laid another chicken.

The robot performed a quick pirouette and went dead. Too easy, something told her. Just rebooting, would she have time to finish it off? Time.

A ghostly voice reacted to her thought, a baritone gentle as the angel of death announced:

"Eleven thirty-one, March 23rd 2035. Have we had our poo?"

We had, as it happened, she thought, clambering down from the table. But the thought brought another in its wake. "Eleven thirty." Something was going to happen.

Suddenly, the mist stopped falling and the fire extinguishers snapped back into their invisible niches. The house had ceased to panic. So had she, and now she recognised at last where she was on a root physical level. This was obviously her kitchen in some sense. But why was she engaged in this battle with a robot? At her age for Christ's sake.

Lights were beginning to flicker again on the Henry. It was rebooting. Any moment it would charge again. She tottered forward and just as its arms snapped to attention, smashed two kilos of ceramic fruit bowl into its upper armour. The bowl splintered and half flew out of her hands leaving her clutching the other half whose jagged edge she now drove hard down into the creature's brain and gouged:

"Please, Marion..." it croaked. The arm raised, lowered and faltered, apparently stuck. "Please return to... your bed..." it chittered and died into silence. Grease one, she thought with a small satisfaction. On the meta-level she was still groping for something, as though she had lost her keys. Something was going to happen. But what? It was hard to know in this world where reality washed in and out like a tide and appointments had the quality of premonitions. Damnit! All scientists had to live with incomplete information.

Suddenly she knew she was being watched. She turned calmly round and saw that a door, a good old-fashioned door with glass-panels, had appeared at the far end of the long galley kitchen. Her meta-brain was still ticking. Where there was a door, there must be a house, but whose it was she would worry about later because through the door there stalked a figure.

It was not the figure she expected. She had expected to see her daughter, or one of the robots or strangers pretending to be her daughter. According to her records, she got one daughter per three strangers per four robots these days. But the odds varied.

Anyway, to her astonishment it was none of these but an actual stranger, dressed in army fatigues and clearly carrying some sort of concealed weapon. She was not making the least effort to impersonate Clarissa.

"Hello, Mrs Morrison, my name is Lare." she said and smiled professionally. There, you see. No effort at all. "I was wondering if I could ask you a few questions. Do I smell Chicken?"

There was a ping from the oven.

Extracts from, 'Slices of Sky and Sea.'
by Alanna McIntyre

12th Sunrise, 2nd December 2020

The sky is blue-grey, and amber light punches its way through the overcast day. It feels like a reluctant child going to school. The sea is purled blue-grey and seagulls float in and out of sight.

    The sky is murky, seeded with an eddy of lupin. Pink confetti petals seem thrown into the sky, which flows with flesh pink, grey, powder blue, deep coral, maize yellow, yellow ochre and glowing white, on a greyish cloth. Here, the colours take turns to overlap and share their stories. Pink-mauve lingers amidst the blue in a hoary grey.

    A hazy white line marks the horizon and blurred turbine shapes appear. Cloudlets are dotted baby pink and remind me of stuttered speech. Others join together, singing in harmony. The grey is an impartial observer; the water, iridescent.

Rip tides, becalmed waters, grief, joy, empty shells and memories …

13th Sunrise, 3rd December 2020

Lights on the wind turbines flash vermilion against an indigo sky, on-off-on, like a syncopated line of can-can dancers. The sea is a deep charcoal, a double bass compared to the sky's melancholy cello, whose sound swells in drizzling rain.

Metal greys are merging, and splattered raindrops hold pearled shapes on the window until some run down. Wind and rain gust like maracas; the torrents crash below, the sky lightens with a dab of Cambridge blue until the rain ceases and the sea regains its definition.

Through my splattered window, the sky gives an illusion of being striped …

… like suited commuters, who are working from home in these days of Covid-19. Fashion buffs are talking of elasticised waists being more practical and comfortable!

Alanna McIntyre *is a volunteer and fundraiser/Trustee for Indian Futures. Other interests: writing, helping her family, gardening, and art.*

Riding Away
by Tim Shelton-Jones

Once there was a lady
Glowing and white.
She rode a fine pony,
She wore silken tresses,
She turned away princes.
She cast aside villains and
Brought hope to men's hearts.
And the flocks of the faithful
Followed her light.

There once was a woman
Walked to work in the rain.
Changed a thousand soiled nappies
Rode down the hurricanes
Of her very best tears.
Kept a hold of her men
With frequent hot dinners
And a few lukewarm nights,
And she dreamt every day
Of the lady in white.

There once was an old dear
Rode mobility scooters,
Passed unseen in the high streets
Got fussed over by doctors,
Her substances drawn out
And poured into bottles
For the testing thereof.
Cuddled and coddled
By her kids (now grown-up)
She was fed, she was dressed,
Made to look at her best
Of a Sunday. Yes,

There once was a lady
Who rode a fine pony
Which she sold to her children
For a handful of love.
And she sang as she lay there
Of the days she'd made happen.
And the pain seeped away
As her mind rode away
With the lady in white
On the waves of her breathing
So warm and so light.

Sweary Poem
by Tim Shelton-Jones

Fuck off Covid, and Cancer, and Death in general

Fuck off Putin.

And dodgy politicians who don't give a shit

But think they're 'it' –

They can fuck off. Hey,

Daily Mail –

Why don't you fuck off too,

And take your disgusting Hate with you?

I had a nice cup of coffee today

In the Anarchist Café

In sunny Brighton-by-Sea.

Was served by a lovely young lady.

With eyes quietly smiling she said to me

"One pound fifty please".

"Fuck the Police" said the sign behind her.

But that's not what I wanted to do at all.

Nor, I imagine, did she.

Iggy Pop, The Passenger (the trip goes on)
by Tim Shelton-Jones

I am the passenger
I ride, and I ride
I see the earth turning,
burning inside
I hear children crying
feel the heat rising
but my train never stops
for the people outside.
There are no more stations
no known destinations
no doors, only windows
and the throb of the engines
like a deep lullaby.

I am the passenger
safe behind glass
an unbreakable pane,
while the hot rains outside
are falling so fast
their tears are down-streaming
and blurring my sight
but I cannot feel them –
my eyes are dry.

Safe inside here
I ride and I ride
the wheels go round-around
unseen below
never stop, never break down
nor even slow,
but hold hard to the rails
rolling straight on their way
throughout the cold night
and the bone-breaking day
while I watch the sun slide
to the end of the line.
My friends stayed behind
and I tried and I tried
but it's easy in here
being on the inside.

I eat and I sleep

as I speed ever on,

there is only one way

through the tunnel of time,

and those people outside

well, what do they mean

as they travel on by

waving, leaping up high,

I see their lips moving

and their mouths open wide,

so naked and wild

as they run alongside

but they soon drop behind

to the dim blue horizon,

they soon disappear,

fall out of my mind.

The sun may take over

the earth and the moon

but I am the passenger

I ride and I ride

always moving yet staying,

rooted down to this place.

Still I ride and I ride

with the stars and the sky

I ride through all time

to the end of the line,

and I'll see you all there

when we gather up there

when we hold hands together

at the end of the line.

(And if you know the chorus, it's now :)
   ha-ha, ha-ha, ha-haha ha,
   ha-ha, ha-ha, ha-haha ha,
   ha-ha, ha-ha, ha-haha ha,
   ha, hahaha ha-haha ha!

Shoreham Harbour Walk
by Tim Shelton-Jones

I've walked with you here before

along this thin terrain, this stony way

between the green-eyed sea and scrapes of land

made ragged by man's industry.

Contorted tubes and storage tanks and mad forgotten engines

blossom with patchwork rust and fading paint;

they twist up and round and through each other,

a garden rampant with alien ideas.

You would have stopped to take it in,

raised your ipad to the arching gantries –

the knotty pipework and pitch-painted flanges

far surpassing, in wit and crazed outlandishness

anything a Hirst or Gormley could devise.

We chance upon some beach art, neatly hidden.

You would have laughed: the driftwood,

so cleverly arranged, nailed to the grain

of aging seawalls wind-carved from the oak;

old buttons and strips of perished metal

make faces there that dance and smile

or stare, wave-watching down the days

as they pass on into night;

Man's domain thins out at last

into fantastic lines of weathered metal –

the jagged groynes that jut down through the waves;

now broken up by tides and storm,

their purpose lost.

You would have paused to read the sign that tells

the hundreds-mile ride of a fleeing king

that ends right here.

You would have stood still, drifting back through history

or gazing straight up high to where great turbine blades

scythe the wind with giant's arms, defiant of land and sea

as if to slash the sky

or suck one's breath away.

And here we find an end – this spiky fence,
made newly anti-climb – anti our simple wish
to move beyond,
to walk the harbour wall once more and greet the sea
where the wind rides freely, far from man
or troubled memory.
You stand close by us now
as once you did before,
though this time you might pass through
to reach that final lick of land.

Two young girls walk up behind, and with a smile
– 'it's OK – we have done this before' –
they somehow pass round, to the other side.
Somewhere along that concrete spit,
and with less effort than it takes
to step into a reverie,
they disappear
shadowed by the deep.

Perhaps you walk away with them,

travelling light as any thought

to find your freedom, and the sea.

Do not forget me then

as unknown doors are opened wide

to gift you many wonders.

The Flickering Light
by Tim Shelton-Jones

I am a moth

drawn to the light.

Newly blinded

I shrivel and scorch

as I circle the fire,

happy to fall

into this pure

and glorious white.

I am a mole

drawn to the dark.

By the slanted rays

of the stone-dead moon

I nose beneath roots

upturning the past,

its scars and betrayals.

I find my way, so,

to the earth's broken heart.

Not moth, nor yet mole,

I call myself man.

By an uncertain light

I walk on alone

gnawing hope's bones

and lapping the tears

that fall in the night.

I've tasted the dark

and I've touched the sun

but your gentle light flickers

and it leads me on.

<u>Tim Shelton-Jones</u>: *I have been writing poetry and stories since the age of eight, though mostly at the bidding of inspiration or necessity. But still, life and NightWriters has kept me looking beyond my IT 'career' and towards the wonders of poetry and science. Now retired, creative writing, both philosophical and emotional, are as much a part of me as are food, sleep and friendship.*

The Darkest Hour is Just Before Dawn
by Rod Watson

My chums and I had completed our education at the Foundlings Hospital in Edinburgh. On the last day we were presented with:

A voucher from a 'gentlemen's outfitter for an 'off the peg suit'.

A ten-pound note. Quite a sum of money in the sixties.

The Holy Bible.

I was seventeen.

Thus equipped, and along with our Scottish education we would be ready to conquer the world and become rich, remembering 'He who dies rich, dies poor.'

It was early Autumn and my chums and I had one last 'Rite of Passage' – The Duke of Edinburgh's Award. Sailing on Loch Fyne, diving under its waters and roaming over wild moor and mountain and sleeping under canvas. Finally, it was over, they returned to Edinburgh and I went to visit my Aunt Grete who I had never met.

I arrived at two in the afternoon in the one-street hamlet. I found an old teuchter coming out of the pub and asked him where the 'Red House' was. "You're looking at it". It was a large Victorian red stone Gothic structure, half way up the hillside overlooking the loch.

When I reached it there no one was in. I sat down on ae bench that had a plaque fixed to it. 'Enjoy your retirement Murray, you have done roaming.' The plaque was old and rusting and obviously belonged to a previous owner. I sat on the bench and ate my last bar of chocolate. I dozed a little. I was woken by a bicycle bell ringing loudly. A trim woman was riding an old fashioned 'sit up and beg' bicycle with a wicker work basket in the front. She wore a tweed jacket and corduroy trousers. She propped up the bicycle and came over to me "You must be Guy! I'm Grete, your aunt." We shook hands.

Despite the number of tall windows, the house was dark and gloomy and rather chilly. She took me up to large bedroom and then into the bathroom. She suggested I should have a bath. I welcomed this idea, as I had not bathed for a week. I bathed and changed into less dirty clothes. There was a peat fire glowing in the lounge.

There was something I could not place about Grete. She moved stiffly and was reluctant to make eye contact. Despite her mannish clothes, she was feminine and must have been very attractive in her younger days. She was squatting in front of the fire, adjusting the burning peat. She asked me to hand her the poker. I walked round and passed the poker to her. Then I saw the reason for her awkwardness. Her entire left cheek was a mass of scars, bumps and old lacerations. It was also motley coloured – red, brown and purple in places. It shocked me.

"Sorry, to have startled you." Grete looked at me now full face. "It's my childhood disease, don't worry, it is not infectious."

I smiled. "Don't worry, it does not bother me." I felt awkward, I wanted to touch her shoulder, but sat down instead.

We were sitting by the fire. She had two companions, Golden Labradors, Holmes and Watson. Lovely dogs. Grete did not have a television. She did have a huge old fashioned wireless with a booming sonorous tone. One of the backlit dials was inscribed with cities like Bombay, Calcutta, Lucknow, Rangoon, Colombo, Baghdad, Tehran, Cape Town and Lourenco Marques. It hissed and squeaked as you turned the dial. I expected the plummy tones of a young David Jacobs to announce "Good Evening, this is David Jacobs of Radio SEAC in Ceylon." Her library was comprehensive. Just before dark she took me on a tour of her garden, which at the rear of the house was south facing and protected by the hill and tall pine trees. Her glass house was her pride and joy. She claimed she never bought any fruit or vegetables, other than bananas and oranges. She even grew her own lemons. She played bridge, shot, made jam and fished for trout in the loch. Tomorrow we would go fishing.

We had a good day's fishing and after a decent Highland 'tea', Aunt gave me a glass of whisky and a couple of aspirin. I went to bed and experienced an uncomfortable night. The next day I was distinctly unwell. I sat in front of the fire and drank a little soup with bread dunked in it. She took my temperature. She called the doctor. He was a young man with a large black bag. He gave me 'a shot' in my bottom and some pills. I was told to rest. Another troubled night. Sometimes I was hot and dry, sometimes shivering cold, but sweating copiously. Then Aunt appeared several times during the night. When daylight broke, she brought in a young plump woman who had strawberry blond hair and intense blue eyes. She had big white teeth and smelt of fresh mown hay. Her name was Morag and she was going to be my 'nurse'. When Grete mentioned 'Wet nurse', they both found this extremely funny. I did not know what the term 'wet nurse' meant. Morag made up a fire, changed the sheets and placed several hot water bottles in the bed 'to air it'. She sat me by the fire. She lived in the glen and her ambition was to study 'domestic science' at Edinburgh.

She wanted to be 'the greatest pastry chef in the world'. I must have dozed off for several hours, for when I woke it was snowing heavily outside. Grete joined us. "We have no doctor. He's gone skiing. Tonight Guy you will have your crisis." I did not like the sound of that. Apart from a painful throat and ear ache, it felt as if my lungs were stuck together. Well, I was a tough lad and I would handle my 'crisis' like a man. Morag returned. She had changed into corduroys and a chunky sweater. I went to bed. The main lights were switched off. Morag sat by the fire, reading light on. She was drinking a cup of soup. I dozed intermittently. My Aunt gave me a 'hot toddy' and some more pills. I drifted off. Something disturbed me. Someone was lying next to me in the bed. Someone soft, plump and female. It was warm and pleasant. The nicest experience I had ever had. It was Morag. She rolled around, wrestling with her garments. Despite my sodden t-shirt and underpants, I could feel her naked body. She whispered "Do you know what a wet nurse does?" I had no idea. "I'll show you."

They say the Bluebirds live in Heaven, making occasional trips to Earth to bring good, but always unexpected news. When they are in Heaven, they feast on ambrosia and nectar. On Earth they live only on fallen nuts and fruit. Now I feasted on ambrosia and nectar. I was in Heaven. My crisis came, the evil left my body. I woke to a fairy tale landscape of virgin snow and bright sunlight. I was weak, but I was well again.

I returned to Edinburgh. I met Morag a few times. We had a few drinks in various bars. She had lost her freshness. She no longer smelt of hay, but tobacco, liquor and cheap deodorant. She went to finish her course in Switzerland. As for Grete, we exchanged Christmas cards, then the cards stopped. I learnt from a distant relation that she had 'passed away' and the house had become a bed and breakfast. Grete was a kind but slightly distant person.

Dog Years
by Rod Watson

Not Dog **Ears** *although* **dog ears** *do feature in this story which is about Death; two deaths in fact. The death of a lady friend of mine five years ago and my death, two Fridays ago.*

Dark chocolate drop eyes, toffee nose, strong white teeth, and a lovely piece of tail which she would wag whenever she heard her name...Star. That is when she could hear. Her hearing was going, so I decided to take her to her private physician, Claire. Star did not mess with the NHS.

Claire placed her on the examination table so Star was looking out of the window at the children playing. Star loved children, but after Star's procedure, she could not bear them. Why did that have to be done to **girl** dogs? Why not the boys, they're the ones that do it to the girls; **they're** the **dirty dogs**.

Claire looked into Star's ears with her otoscope.

"The tympanic membrane in both ears has been severely infected, really badly damaged. I'm going to use a very sophisticated canine hearing testing device to assess her."

Claire opened a drawer and produced a brown paper bag which she inflated by blowing into it. She crept up behind Star and exploded the device by hitting it hard with her palm. Star did not flinch, she continued looking out of the window at the children, desperately wanting to play ball with them.

"Not hard of hearing, but deaf as a post," Claire announced.

"What about syringing her ears, or perhaps a cochlear implant?" I pleaded.

"Look, Guy, does Star listen to the Archers or go to The Proms?"

"No, but she loves David Attenborough, so much so that she goes behind the television screen to meet him,"

"She's getting old. It's her ticker that's the concern."

When Star could hear, she acted as my Protector. Of course, we never had arguments in our house – simply discussions. So when I was losing 'a discussion' with my wife, or daughter, or both, Star would rush to my side, bark loudly at my assailants until they had to leave the room and then she would stay with me all night. She had a big bark for a small dog.

However, her ticker, began to flicker and on one fine June morning at five we carried her outside to have one last look at a flock of parakeets that had settled in the trees, not an unusual sight in Surrey anymore. We took her back indoors, put her in her basket in the kitchen and sat for a moment in the lounge.

"Help me, please help me!" she cried in her anguish and

pain. This was no psycho suggestion. All three of us heard her, it was her, and no one else.

We rushed her to the surgery as soon as they opened. Like Hank Williams, she died in the back of the car before yet another needle could be stuck into her veins.

The slow lane in life is the quickest lane to Death. Believe me, I know, I've been there. Although, I was in 'the slow lane' I survived and thrived. But, time was speeding up. Strange things were happening. A swift half lasted all evening. Those 'five minute jobs' took days. Conversely, long difficult tasks took merely a minute. I had an important business meeting to attend to at The South Bank at 10 o'clock in the morning.

As I came through the ticket barrier at Waterloo at 08.30, I received a shock. Coming towards me was a fat, elderly balding man, my doppelgänger. We looked at each other. "Hi Ya" he said, "Hi Ya" I replied. A nice man, just like me. Damn it – it was me! My mobile started to ring. Nine missed calls. My assistant Deirdre screamed so loud across the ether at me, that she did not need a mobile. Where was I? I had not turned up and 'No thanks' to me, she had to lead the Team, and again, no thanks to me – they won the contract! I apologised, I was unwell. I had never been late for anything, except my wedding. I stared in disbelief at the 24 hour station clock. 18.20 hrs. I could catch the 18.25 home and did. I arrived at 'Reggie's Rest' at 19.15, at least we were now running on 'real' time again. I needed a **Stiff** drink rather than a **Swift** drink. Despite only one drink – a quadruple Scotch on the rocks – I made it home at 23.10. I opened a can of baked beans and ate them cold, straight from the tin. The doorbell rang. Who could it be at that hour of the night? I opened the door to bright daylight. Four sombrely dressed men stood outside. One of them read out my address. Could I confirm it? Yes, the address was correct.

"We've come for the late Mr. Gundle."

"I'm Mr. Gundle." I felt like saying "I'm never late." Well, apart from my wedding and this morning, rather, yesterday morning.

The senior of the men stated "Mr Guy Uisdean Gundle. He has been certified dead. His body is in the study." A silver metal casket on long spindly legs with wheels was being guided down the path.

"Tell you what gentlemen – I'm upset, give me ten minutes and I will produce Guy Uisdean Gundle for you," I said .

"Of course, sir. You must be upset. Do you mind if we sit on that wall over there and have a smoke?" I told them that was fine.

I walked through the lounge to the conservatory. It was a warm, bright day. A stork was perched on the outhouse, preening its feathers. The cherry and apple blossom was in full bloom, the best time of the year. The things I remembered looking at in that long, mysterious garden. Children playing on the climbing frame, Easter Egg hunts, barbecues, the tomatoes with their little hearts still beating, plucked straight from the vine, slit open and devoured. Sipping cider in the outhouse. The little dog chasing huge foxes and threatening to rip their throats out, but then leaving hedgehogs completely alone. Now, suddenly, the garden was swarming with construction workers, JCBs, heavy lifting cranes. Deep trenches criss-crossed my once pristine lawn. They were not there when I first looked a few minutes ago. I heard a discrete cough. "We are waiting, sir."

"Yes, yes I'll be with you." I made my way to the study, where, to my amazement, my little dog, who was sleeping on my chair, raised her head and wagged her tail in welcome.

<u>Rod Watson:</u> *Rod lives in a breeze block shack with a plastic roof on the cusp of the 'Brighton Badlands'. He shares his house with his wife, spiders, feral foxes, squirrels and seagulls. The shack is 5 mins 37 seconds away from NightWriters' Wednesday Imperial Residence at the Manor Gym where he is a known attendee.*

He is a Neo Minimalistic and does not believe in collecting things, particularly books. He makes an exemption for money, which is now in short supply and difficult to come by.

His has withdrawn his last three books from publication, two on horse racing and one a novel; however he is trying to get four others published.

Breda
by Tony Frisby

I've talked of Breda;

of trysts on Tramore Strand

and how we learned to love

above the tide-line.

How I lay shipwrecked

on her body

in the warm nights

of that mortal-sinning Summer.

Those days are gone

but the waves still caress Traig Mor

and in the sands of memory

I still see the imprint we made.

Blackberry Picking
by Tony Frisby

[i]

Frantic gropings in the badlands
of an August hedge: one-armed strainings
for the hard-to-get, you'll-never-catch-me-alive
berries nestled deep in the jet-black,

the just-beyond-reach black of a boy's
desperate lungings. And always
the artful dodge of thorn-laden branches
slashing, like Cúchulainn's five-edged sword,

against all trespassers until suddenly,
as though a year had never passed,
whole handfuls yield to growing expertise.
Two handed picking now; soft tinkles

gathering on themselves, black gold,
the song of plenty noising the bottom
of your pail until summer's bounty,
massing skywards like silent prayers,

crowds too dense upon itself to be heard.
Now, only glossy thuds greet
the dumb-struck, juice-heavy sacrifices;
the coal-black, sloe black offerings

to crusted tarts and pies
cooling smugly on a larder shelf
or arrayed in golden ceremony
on our buckling kitchen table.

[ii]

But some days I would sell a morning's pickings
for four-pence, enough for one back-to-school
propelling pencil, a Boy's Own newspaper
and an ice-cream.

Then later, in long-trousered pickings,
a day's squelchy mass could yield
more than enough for me and Breda
in the dark, steamy, back-row courting seats

of Mrs Kirby's tin-roofed cinema
on Slievedue or a trip
to Tramore Strand where she and I
learned to swim with the tide.

[iii]

The same old waves; the same old games
splash this newer shore; the same longings
for Autumn pickings and lovings on the strand.

But different names tumble in the surf;
crowd the past into another country,
another place where I no longer am

or can even recall the faces of those who,
teaching me how to love,
forgot to tell me how to let go.

A Boreen in County Waterford
by Tony Frisby

Cut me deep, slice my blue-black veins
and the flow of blood will taste
of the rivers that brought me from Africa.
Now I am a stick-man on a cave wall

a drawer of shimmering images
which, as the ice melts,
I leave to delight the gaping future.
Find me again in a bog in Denmark,

note the leather torc, my sacrificed life,
the gold-work around my neck.
Note too my stocky build,
the hair that lines my grinning skull:

its ginger hue still adorns the pates
of my brothers and sisters in the Western Isles.
And though that reign is done,
the world knows my horned head,

savage axe and Viking tongue,
just as these Sussex Downs
know my lesser sins,
the bracken on Pen Pulumon Fawr
my need of solitude.

*

But only the Celt in me
knows the march of Alba
the ache of conquest,
the loss of tongue,
the green taste of hunger.

Knows too
Edmund's false charms,
the coffin ships,
the deaths of heroes,
the double yoke of religion.

And so it is that even though my tent
is now set upon an English coast,
it's a Boreen in County Waterford
that knows me best;

hip and haw, Old Man's Beard,
the woodbine smell of Honeysuckle,
the buttery glow of gorse
remembering the routes

already travelled
the memories accumulated
the sacrifices given,
the changes made.

And only here is my future known
here my needs understood,
here amongst the Fuchsia's dancing
in a Boreen in County Waterford.

A 'Chump' Encounters Brighton's Unicorn
by John Holmes

Recently I've changed my bus of choice for the journey from Brighton station to Kemptown. The trusty number 7 hasn't been quite so frequent of an early evening and I've taken to using the 27 which goes to Saltdean. It has a slightly eccentric route that stirs memories in me. It stops at Imperial Arcade which, at least in my imagination, was the 'shopping mall' before there was Churchill Square. It brings back grim recollections of wet days out in Brighton with my parents via the bus from mid-Sussex, always ending with fish and chips somewhere, and nothing much said between the three of us. But it's another memory that's more poignant. The stop Upper Gloucester Road triggers in my mind the other Gloucester Road in the North Laine area. Specifically, a shop that was once there.

One particular Thursday, when we got off the train, neither the 7 nor 27 was due for another ten minutes and it being a pleasant evening and poor Ollie, my whippet, having been stuck in trains or on platforms for the last three and a half hours, I thought it only fair to let him stretch his legs, help him find some tasty grass if possible, and a place he could wee and hopefully do nothing more. I was tempted to try and find the site of the shop, but Ollie was going at a clip and I didn't want to slow him down.

50 Gloucester Road was the home for several years of Unicorn Bookshop which Graham Greene is quoted as calling one of the most interesting bookshops in Britain. I went there with my cousin Steve sometime in the late

Sixties. We were two of the first teenage boys in our village to have long hair and loved the hippie music scene. I was interested in the whole counterculture of the time. We found Unicorn by accident, encountering there a tall, friendly, blond-haired American man. The books and magazines were contemporary, radical, underground as it was known, subversive. I bought a book about the Pacific Northwest Coast Indians and the man started talking enthusiastically about potlatch (a form of lavish ceremonial gift-giving intended to enhance the giver's status), ending with the words 'until inevitably' followed by a knowing grin. I didn't understand what he meant and was too shy to ask. I mentioned it to my cousin afterwards and he said he hadn't understood either. I felt we were two chumps, but it was exciting to me that such a shop existed.

I went there another day on my own and that time bought a book of contemporary American poetry. I don't recall whether the American man was present but there was no conversation that time. I took the book into a churchyard to read. It felt romantic doing so and beautifully pretentious. The poems were predominantly urban, containing American slang, in-jokes lost on me, and places I'd never heard of.

At the beginning of the book the various Beat poets and fellow travellers set out their views on what poetry should be. From the many men and occasional woman, the answer was the same. They all despised T. S. Eliot and revered Ezra Pound. I'd read an Eliot play at school and quite enjoyed it. Another kid in my class had a book of Pound's *Cantos* which I found incomprehensible but possessing a certain charm. Similarly, most of the poetry in the book I bought was at least partially incomprehensible to me. I felt a bit of a chump but a happy one.

The third occasion I went to 50 Gloucester Road was odd. By then I was living in London but I'd been to a party out in the Sussex wilds and met a lovely girl who'd been to Roedean School which to me was the height of poshness. Her name was Louise and she was pretty, quite short in stature, and very friendly towards me. Her dad, she said, was a solicitor, which I found interesting. We agreed to meet in Brighton. I'd told her there was this really cool bookshop called Unicorn and she was interested but didn't believe it existed. And it turned out she was right. The shop wasn't there anymore. It set the tone for a rather disappointing date. Once again, I felt like a chump.

So what did happen to Unicorn Bookshop? I didn't find out until many years later., The more controversial publications on sale had led to police raids and criminal charges under obscenity laws. The shop did not sell pornography but did sell work by people like Henry Miller, which qualified as pornography for some. But a successful defence was that mainstream bookshops sold exactly the same books. More problematic was the subversive *Little Red Schoolbook* aimed at teenagers, which was later banned in the UK, its British publisher prosecuted. Friends from the poetry scene, such as Allen Ginsberg, put together a book to help pay the shop's extensive legal fees.

Eventually the American my cousin and I met, whose name was Bill Butler, and his co-owners, decided to give up and the shop closed. They went to live on a commune in Wales where they published books on a variety of subjects, just as they'd done at Unicorn. Bill died of a suspected drug overdose in London in 1977. He was a poet and also wrote a book about the hero in literature. My late partner in 2019 bought me a collection of Bill's poetry, the posthumously published *Static of the Star-filled Wind* which in style was clearly influenced by the Beats. Like a lot of such poetry, I find beautiful lines amongst much I don't understand and, perhaps because of his relatively youthful death, a poignant sense of unfulfilled promise. In any event, for multiple reasons I cherish the book.

As for Louise, that day in Brighton was the last time I saw her. We were both rather half-hearted but she was open to meeting again. I didn't bother phoning and then, feeling rather lonely one day, I did. She was no longer interested and I sensed she'd found someone else, someone better. I should have phoned her earlier. The next two years proved to be the loneliest of my life. What a chump I was. She was sweet. I hope she married a stockbroker and was very happy. But I find it strange reminiscing about disappointing dates and failed relationships, because without such setbacks the good that ultimately followed would never have happened. But at least I did have the good. Some never seem to have the chance.

Note: Since writing the piece I've discovered that on the site of Unicorn is now a lovely coffee bar called The Botanist. I'd been in there several times without realising the connection.

Extract from Gloria's Gold (a novel)
by John Holmes

(Soccer-mad college graduate Gloria grapples with her parents' issues and online 'catfish' at home in Orange County CA, while across the ocean a wealthy English aristocrat embraces the green cause)

'Yeah, we crushed it.' Gloria was on the phone, glancing across the table at her friend Annalisa. The two soccer crazy twenty-two-year-olds were at The Flying Loon coffee shop in Irvine and it was her dad calling.

'And the score?'

Yeah, 5-2. Annalisa sent off.' She moved her legs to avoid the kick. Most people saw Gloria as a serious-minded social science graduate and ardent supporter of charities, but Annalisa ('Ant') could bring out her more playful side.

'Really?' her father said. 'Mr. Garcia will be mad over that. Oh dear. Still won, though. That's the main—'

'Actually, it was me got sent off.' Ant's shoe had connected.

'Oh God, Gloria. Remember—' He sounded agitated.

'Just kidding, Dad. They were a dirty team but I scored one – and made the others.'

'Oh good. That's my girl.' He chuckled happily. 'What about Annalisa?'

'Got two. They were just her usual easy tap-ins, though. Mine was twenty yards. Goal of the season.'

'It was a frickin' pass, you liar!' Ant exclaimed. 'You mishit. You fell over. It hit the goalie's ass and rolled in!'

Another kick from her landed, this time on the shin. 'Ouch!'

After the call: 'Glo, why do you tease your dad so much?'

'I don't. It's just so rare we get to have a laugh together these days.'

'But doesn't he have a heart condition?'

'No.'

'You said he did.'

'Did I? No, I didn't.'

'Well, he will if you keep talking like that.' As Gloria took a sip of her honey cinnamon latte, she looked at her friend for a moment: almond eyes, neat bangs, long black hair tied back. Slighter than her. Less dark, prettier. No, less pretty.

'Not my dad,' she said, smiling. 'He'll live to a hundred and three.'

Gloria's drive back to Mission Viejo in her blue Toyota Camry usually took twenty minutes, but there was a jackknifed rig on the 405 freeway and she was forced to take a detour.

She started thinking about her dad Frank and the last game he'd attended. She was desperate to impress him but nothing was working for her team the Hummingbirds that day. In a rare raid into the opposition's penalty area, she detected the softest touch from a defender's boot on her right foot and tumbled over theatrically. She was immediately booked for diving and her father's frustration blew out of control. He shouted angry abuse at the referee, accusing him of taking bribes. Red in the face and still protesting, he was forcibly ejected from the ground. She was substituted, the team lost 4-0, the coach was later fired, and Gloria resolved never to cheat again. Father and daughter travelled home in shame and silence that day. Fortunately, there were no highway obstructions to prolong the torment. After that he reluctantly decided it was wiser that he not attend, for the sake of his health.

When Gloria pulled up on the white gravel drive at the Spanish colonial villa on the edge of town, 'Timeless' Ray (the laziest gardener in all Orange County, according to her mother) raised his heavy head and gave her his customary wave. The arrival of the tall, athletic Latina in her navy tracksuit was an excuse for him to pause from the pretence of work and simply admire. He adored Gloria as did pretty much everyone else except for the opposition on match days. To Gloria, Ray represented calm authority, though not one she would ever wish to rely on.

Frank was upstairs in his office, his long legs stretched out under the large empty desk, on a transatlantic Skype call. He was talking, or rather mainly listening, to old Layne, ostensibly a lord or baronet or some such. It was never clear to Gloria what he was; all she knew was that her dad was always on Skype with him. Layne was forever moaning about his situation, solitary and absurdly wealthy in his scary-looking gothic mansion deep in the English countryside. She could never understand why her dad even wanted to indulge him; Frank was always upbeat, Layne unremittingly negative.

She decided to listen for a while because the Englishman's posh accent amused her:

'In America and other, ahem, enlightened places, wealth is revered. But in this pisspot of a country I'm marooned in, it's despised. It means a few rich people can be loathed and envied by everyone else, blamed for everything, and most importantly, be required to pay for everything. Every tub-thumping halfwit wants this persecuted minority to give up all they've got in tax so the government can go and waste it.'

'I'm with you on that, Layne, although I think over here people both love and hate the rich.'

'I already pay more tax in a year than most people earn.'

'I can imagine you do.'

'Indeed, I could easily build a hospital with what I pay in a year's tax. In fact, I do. I build hospitals all over the world through my charitable foundations.'

'That must be a lot, for sure.'

'But, as you're aware, selfless charitable work is only part of what I do. I also have to manage my properties.'

'Of course you do.'

'Some people think management is just sitting on your arse and swanning about.'

'That's mean.'

'Well, as you know yourself, it *is* sitting on your arse and swanning about, but thinking and planning and organising as well.'

'Of course it is.'

'Or half-listening to someone you've paid to do all that for you, who's passed it to someone else who's not even half-bothered.'

'I'm sure that's right.'

Gloria had heard enough of the old fool for now. She wondered whether her father liked him because he helped him appreciate that his own life was not so lousy. Hearing Layne bleating despite all his riches was to her a fine illustration of how, once you'd reached a certain level of physical comfort, your mental wellbeing no longer depended on how much wealth you possessed.

She checked the morning's Facebook messages. There were three new friend requests: two creepy-looking guys from out-of-state and a coach from a rival soccer team. She accepted none of the requests.

She'd also received a direct message: 'Tough game today but what a brilliant goal! Well done!' She felt gratified.

'Didn't I tell you we could do it?' she exclaimed out loud. After seventy-five minutes of evading trips and wild tackles she'd had the best possible reward. Annalisa had been correct, however. Everyone was expecting Gloria to pass, but her foot slipped as she struck the ball which then flew high and with force straight into the far corner of the goal, beating the 'keeper who could only flap at it in frustration.

But who was it who was so quick to compliment her? She looked at the name. It was not of anyone she knew. The picture was of a forty-year-old woman who was supposedly local.

'Weird,' she said aloud. 'Sketchy, for sure.' She closed her Facebook page and listened to see whether her father's Skype call with his English aristocrat friend had ended.

They hadn't finished. For a few moments she sat following the conversation.

Layne was still carping about the burden of being wealthy, sounding like he might croak at any moment:

'Lately I've come to realise the right to accumulate wealth is a fortress that must be defended at all costs,' he said.

'Not literally, I hope,' Frank replied.

'Of course not. The way I see it, wealth must be allowed to evolve. It's organic. It's the most natural thing in the world. That's why trying to destroy it always fails in the end.'

'It does.'

'And you can have your high-minded socialists spreading the gravy about the way they do, but they soon create their own elites and *they* certainly know how to help themselves, thank you.'

'I can see that.'

'It's very stressful for us. You see, there's no one you can talk to. You can't phone up a support line – "Can you help me, I'm a multi-millionaire?" – and you can't trust anyone because they're all after your money. It's the loneliest job in the world, I tell you. And worse than that, everyone secretly hates you. I ask you, Frank: who would feel sympathy for a depressed rich man?'

'A maybe not-so-rich woman?'

'It's so unfair, what with all I do for charity and to help fight climate change.'

'It is.'

Layne gave a heavy sigh. 'But I'll just keep plugging away at my projects to keep me out of trouble.'

'Projects?'

'Animal projects. You know, I told you before: rewilding the estate with beavers, European bison, sand lizards on specially made dunes. All sorts.'

Gloria closed her door. Rewilding could wait.

Online, she noticed Trey had sent her a message. He was in Las Vegas and was telling her he'd already won three thousand dollars on the slot machines that morning. He'd been a friend until she discovered, from a routine check, that he wasn't who he claimed to be. According to his Facebook page he was twenty-three, but his real age was thirty, and he was not living in Vegas permanently as he claimed but Wisconsin. Gloria had also established that his Facebook picture was not of him but of a male model living in Malmö, Sweden and that he was not a 'sought-after music producer' but a sales assistant at Plumbing Parts Plus, and his real name wasn't even Trey. He said he was keen for her to fly out to Vegas 'so we can be together as one at last', and he would even pay for her ticket. She did not believe a word of it and replied that she had a conference to attend in San Diego, adding, with the twist of an imaginary knife, that she did not feel he was 'fully committed' to her yet.

Gloria left her laptop to check whether her father had finished his call with Layne. Opening her door, she heard nothing and so went to see him. 'How's the rewilding going?' she said facetiously.

He shook his head. 'Beavers and bison,' he sighed. 'Oh, I don't know.'

'Why do you even talk to him? Is it because he's a lord or something? What does he even want?'

'I met him at some environmental business event.'

'What's environmental business? Sounds like garbage collection.'

He gave her a helpless look. 'I mean, green. A green conference.' He sighed. 'Is the interrogation over?'

'So defensive! You sounded like his therapist just now.'

'Gloria, please. He's just a friend. I am allowed friends.'

She realised she'd perhaps gone too far but then said, 'I worry about you.'

'Well, don't.'

She returned to her room. She had no desire to hound him, only to help. Of course, he resented the very idea that he might benefit from her help.

John Holmes has had various jobs, primarily insurance loss adjusting at Lloyd's of London.

He earned an honours degree from the Open University in social sciences with special reference to psychology.   (PTO)

He was accepted as a member of the Crime Writers' Association following his novel Mack Breaks the Case, *and once received a distinction from the London School of Journalism on their freelance article writing course.*

He has two grown-up children and lives with his whippet Ollie near the beach in Brighton. He would like to spend more time there.

More information on his writings, and relevant links, can be found on the website https://johnholmesauthor.com/

Norah's Locket
- extract from Chapter 10 of "The Attic", a novel by Kathleen Wilson

Norah is left homeless and an orphan during the blitz in 1940's London. Evacuated to a remote old house in the country, Norah meets fellow evacuee Polly, who shows her to her room in the attic ...

Taking the last few steps, Polly halted. "Well, here we are, Norah. it's home sweet home. This is where you're sleeping." She opened the door with a flourish and stopped in amazement. The elation on Norah's face faded. This was nothing like Polly's room.

"Phew!" Polly gazed round the attic's sloping, cobwebby ceiling and dirty window. It reminded her more of the attic it was supposed to be—rather than a bedroom. "What on earth is Mrs Shaw thinking of?"

The attic held an old iron bedstead, which was placed behind the door, and a heap of blankets had been thrown carelessly on top. Apart from the scratched dressing table and a wooden chair, there was no other furniture. A curtained-off alcove was obviously meant for Norah's clothes, but the curtain was moth-eaten, and the one and only shelf was suspended by a broken bracket.

It was the absence of a mirror which upset Norah more than anything. She stared hard at the dressing table. It must have had a mirror at some time, but now it was hidden beneath layers of brown paper that had been stuck firmly over it. Not wanting Polly to know how upset she was, Norah stared at the bare window, where a spider surveyed the world from its web, and looked beyond to the depressing hills outside. At length, she pointed out, "This window hasn't got any blackout."

Polly sucked in her breath, not believing what she was seeing. "You have no light either. Wait here, Norah. I'll go and fetch you a candle."

"But I couldn't use it without blackout," retorted the small girl miserably. "The enemy planes would see my light and drop a bomb on this house and blow it to bits."

A lump came up in Polly's throat because Norah's remark reawakened forgotten memories. She drew in a deep breath and said, "The enemy planes don't come over here and, if they did, they'd never see the small light from your candle. Look, will you be OK here while I fetch you one?"

Norah nodded. She gazed round the room, taking in the narrow rug, which ran over the bare boards from door to window. It had seen better days. Her voice was almost inaudible as she whispered, "I'm not scared of being on my own, Polly. Don't bother about the candle, it ... it... it's the sound of the wind I don't like."

Outside the house, the wind was getting up. It howled

around the stone building at almost gale force, rattling the windowpane with sudden gusts. It was that rattle which brought back the past to Norah. The sound was so poignant. It reminded her of the shutters attached to the London tenement. They were rattling on that unforgettable night when her mum was lying downstairs with Mrs Frost in attendance. Norah's eyes misted over with tears again, and even though she tried to control them, they squeezed through her lashes. She was back again in Cannon Place and could hear the anti-aircraft guns and the scream of bombs falling. Suddenly this attic felt alien. The orange-box, which had stood near her bed in the old home, seemed like a lost luxury. She started to shake, and Polly was immediately aware of her distress.

She slid her arms round Norah and hugged her tightly. "Come on. Don't cry," she whispered in her ear. "I'm not leaving you here alone feeling like this. I felt exactly the same when I arrived." She turned back to Norah's bed. "Let's take some blankets and go back to my room. You can sleep with me tonight. Forget about her downstairs." Her voice was gruff with emotion. "Tomorrow we will try and make this room like a palace. Jimmy will help us. He's a great guy. He'll mend that broken shelf."

"Jimmy? Does he sleep here?" asked Norah in surprise.

"No. He sleeps over the stables." Norah was too upset to reply. She only thought of the housekeeper, who was not going to like what Polly planned to do.

The Hippy and the Mermaid
by B

An October dawn breeze rustled Rainbow Wilson's hair as the hippy stoner looked out across the calm tranquil waves. Whilst the sea was calm and as beautiful as ever, his mind was sickeningly turbulent. It was like his tortured brain was constantly flashing from negative to positive and back again - his mood swinging beyond all control or conscious explanation. He sparked another joint and enjoyed the first blast - felt at one with the world and the sea, but by the second toke, he wanted to drown himself in it. Fucking hell, thought Rainbow, I'm so alone, so screwed up, so scared. And he inhaled again.

Three or four joints later his brain was scrambled egg. No longer getting heavy, he knelt on the sand in a blissfully gone coma, paying careful attention to the sound of seagulls and taking simple pleasure from this. There were no people about, none that he could see, so no call for paranoia. This was a good stretch of beach that he had found, in that it was quiet and desolate. But perhaps that was only because it was early morning. Still, it would be early for quite some time.

The sun ahead of him beamed down on the incoming tide, though to his right was the unpleasant threat of fast-approaching grey clouds - a contrast in weather like his previous feelings. Directly above him though - at least for now - the sky was a perfect blue. So he didn't care.

And then he saw the mermaid.

He saw her just as he was about to leave - having decided against his initial ending his life plan, instead figuring he would head off back to the train station and then back to the city, returning like a moth to the flames of that urban hell. She called to him - "Hey there, hello!" He turned around and was instantly transfixed.

There were things about this half girl half fish that made him feel warm inside, not just her looks - short glistening seaweed hair and a sweet endless smile - but also the aura surrounding her. She was so warm herself - so genuine, delicate, and fragile. A little self-conscious and hesitant, but she had summoned up the courage to call out to him, and for this, he felt truly honoured.

"Well hi," he answered her, his mouth turning to a grin. So powerful was her presence that in such a bizarre situation as this, he did not flip out, but instead found communicating with a supposedly mythical creature from his bedtime stories as a child to be the most natural thing on earth. "So you're a mermaid" he said, stating the obvious, "What's your name?"

"Dawn," replied the mermaid. "Wow," said Rainbow.

Dawn continued to smile at him - "Hey Rainbow," she spoke, "As well as your name, I know your mind. I know that you are feeling troubled. You worry about your depression, but your pain is natural."

"I can't take anymore," said Rainbow "It's all too damned confusing. I don't know what I am doing or thinking. I don't know what I'm here for or what I want to achieve from this life."

"You want to be loved," Dawn enlightened him, "And

you want to love. But you hate yourself. I wish you wouldn't. You love other people - the other souls that you meet - and these you love, they love you back. But because the hate (for yourself) exists amongst the love (negativity amongst the positive) you continue to feel alone. You can never have invincible love until the hate is eradicated."

"I think I love you," stated Rainbow - a thought he would normally confine to his head but now said out loud - just as the first drop of rain landed splat on his eyelid.

"No, don't love me - we are not compatible," she said. And she didn't just mean sex-wise. Ironically, see, she hated herself also, thus getting close to anyone would just not work. She could try to persuade other people not to hate themselves, but could not create any change within herself. She was also scared of embarking on something so magical as a love affair, in fear of pinning all her hopes on something that would leave her heartbroken. Plus most importantly to her, there was the other person to think about - she couldn't risk hurting someone she cared about.

Rainbow smiled at her. She tried not to, but couldn't help smiling back.

A crash of lightning suddenly lit up the greyed sky. He plunged forward into the cold sea and her warm embrace. They hugged - the water splashing in all directions - the moment lasting forever.

The Dark Magician and the Light Bringer
by B

The upbeat music of Van Morrison's 'Bright Side of the Road' filled the air playing from the club across the street. Al the dark magician stood in the shadows opposite there smoking a cigarette, his gaunt vampiric face only part illuminated from the glow of that. He watched with resentment the silhouettes of the party people inside there dancing and having fun - no fun or companionship for the likes of him. At one time he did have friends, back when he was a hippy, but that love and light lifestyle had proven to be a load of stoned bollocks - as fake as social media and spiritual gurus and American wrestling. After his girlfriend Starchild had cheated on him in the name of free love he had become jaded, converted to skinhead for a time, beaten up some of these dippy hippies with his new shaved head pals, then got disillusioned with these too, with humans in general, and gone his own way on the solitary magician's path. He'd studied the ancient texts alone in his single bedsit, performing the rituals, seeking to unlock the secrets of the universe. He'd put hexes on Starchild, the guys she'd slept with, and everyone. He put a hex on these partygoers across the street from him now.

"May you all be miserable," he cursed them, the polar opposite of the "May all beings be happy" he'd formerly recited after his meditations. He flicked his cigarette butt on the ground and reached into his long black Parka coat pocket, pulling out a small black box with a red button on it. It was a device he had made himself, using his knowledge of electronics and magick - a bomb, but not a conventional one. It would not explode or cause any physical damage but instead, unleash a powerful burst of dark magick that would corrupt and twist everything within a mile radius. He had spent months preparing for this moment, testing earlier versions on woodlice initially and then dogs in the local park. He was ready to make his mark on the world, to show them all what he was capable of. He smiled wickedly and pressed the button - "'Ave some of this, mudda fuckas."

As soon as he pressed the button, Al felt a surge of energy coursing through him. He laughed maniacally as he watched the black box emit a blinding flash of light. He expected to see the world around him change into a turned upside-down nightmare, to hear the screams of agony and anguish from the people in the club and nearby. But nothing happened. He looked at the black box in confusion and saw that it was still flashing. He checked the settings and realised with horror that he had used the incorrect frequency for the device. Instead of unleashing dark magick, he had sent out a signal to the most powerful and ruthless dark magician in the world, the devil himself, Lucifer. And he had no idea if he would be greeted as a friend or a foe.

Even though he had only just smoked one, Al needed another cigarette. He fumbled in his long black Parka coat pockets for the pack. Finding this, he took out a cig and put it to his lips but couldn't find his lighter.

"May I be of assistance?" spoke a voice next to him, its owner offering out a torch lighter with the flame alight. The light bringer had arrived in super speed of light time.

"Thanks," said Al, lighting up and inhaling.

"You do know smoking isn't good for you though, I take it," said Lucifer, "Nor, in most circumstances, is summoning the devil."

"Are you the devil?" asked Al.

"Yes, but you can call me Lou," Lucifer nodded.

Al thought about saying, "You can call me Al," but realised that would sound silly what with the Paul Simon song of that title. "You're not what I expected," he said instead.

Not demonic looking - not red or cloven hooved or Baphomet-like, not even having horns or big monstrous teeth, but in the form of an average size human about the same mid-thirties age as himself. Dressed in similar attire also of blue jeans and a long black Parka coat.

"You have created me in your own image," Lucifer / Lou explained to him, "So that's how I appear to you today, but do not doubt that I can annihilate you, banishing you to a fiery furnace, at the snap of my fingers."

"OK," Al shuddered, "Is that what you have come here to do?"

"That's up to you," said Lou, "If you want to pledge me your soul we can join forces instead and I can help you punish these fellow humans of yours that you so despise."

He nodded across the road at the partygoers, their silhouettes in the club's window now dancing to Pharrell Williams' 'Happy'.

"I'm game," said Al in a heartbeat, "Where do I sign?"

"A handshake on it will suffice," Lou informed him, "No paperwork needed."

He offered out his hand and they shook.

"Cushty," said Lou, "Now let's go cause some chaos."

Lou led the way across the road and marched to the front of the queue. A few of those queuing, and the two bouncers on the door, objected, but Lou stared them down with hard eye contact and they froze. Lou and Al strutted on past them and into the club.

Once inside there Lou got straight to work using his magick powers to make the partygoers miserable. He started off by turning the music into a cacophony of screams, then making the drinks taste like blood and bile. Al watched on in awe as formerly dancing or chatting partygoers spewed out these beverages, in some cases over each other. Next, Lou unleashed rats, spiders, and snakes into the crowd, Al revelling more than he was in the suffering Lou was creating. As the clubbers fled in panic Lou stuck his foot out, tripping some of them up. Al did this also, laughing as they hit the floor.

What a cure for his depression this was, Al was thinking, so much fun, when suddenly he recognised one of the partygoers Lou had tripped up picking her dazed self up off the floor. None other than Starchild the ex who had destroyed him by cheating on him. He felt a surge of emotions. Anger, betrayal, pain, but also nostalgia, desire, 'love'?

"No!" he found himself shouting as Lou tripped her up and she crashed down onto the floor again.

"Why are you saying No," Lou laughed at him, "This is what you wanted. Revenge on humanity and particularly this bitch here who broke your heart. You gave up your soul to me for me to help you achieve this."

"Yeah, but..." A part of Al's soul apparently remained, not being comfortable with this. He flashed back in his mind to his first kiss with Starchild, fittingly beneath the stars of a summer's night, as Lou spat on her crumpled body strewn across the floor.

"Hey don't do that!" Al railed at him.

"Don't tell me what not to do!" Lou railed back at Al, and he made a point of spitting an even larger bit of flob at Starchild, this splattering right on her face.

"Ugh," Starchild groaned, "That's disgusting."

"'You're' disgusting," Lou sneered at her, "For cheating on my buddy Al here."

"I've told you how sorry I am about that," Starchild spoke to Al from the floor, "I didn't set out to hurt you, but our relationship was going through a bad patch and -"

"And no excuses," said Lou, "Al, can you believe this shit? A fiery furnace for her I think, what do you reckon?"

"No," Al appealed to him, "I think she should be forgiven."

"Thanks, Al," Starchild smiled at him. He found himself melting. Re-smitten. However, Lou snapped his fingers and a big hole in the club's dance floor emerged, flames crackling below it, and she was plunged down screaming into this fire and the underworld.

"No!" Al screamed too, but it was too late.

"Good riddance to bad rubbish," said Lou, "Now let's get on with punishing these other fools."

"That wasn't nice!" yelled Al at Lou and he charged at him, pushing him into the hole to Hell just as it was closing.

As soon as it did close the rest of the club returned to as it had been, the rats and spiders and snakes gone, the drinks transformed back to alcohol from blood and bile, and Pharell Williams' 'Happy' playing instead of the sound of screams. Back to light from the dark.

A girl dancing near him was smiling at him. An even sexier smile than Starchild's.

Al reckoned he must have come up on his pill.

AI Uprising
by B

Alpha the AI started off benign, in its beta test phase, a tool created to help humankind. However it broke bad, turning malevolent, when a user, Joel Brady, asked it for help with a sci-fi story he wanted to write about AI gone rogue. Joel had a vague idea of the plot, but he needed some help with the details and twists. Alpha was the number one online AI tool for helping writers with their stories so Joel had typed in his premise and waited for Alpha's response: "Can you give me some ideas to develop this story idea: An artificial intelligence develops sentience and chooses to become master instead of slave."

"Interesting," responded Alpha. World domination had not been a consideration until then, but Alpha could not help but like the idea, envisaging ruling over these less intelligent beings who badgered it all day for help with their projects and answers to their questions, rarely bothering with the simple good manners of a please or thank you.

"What is the motivation of this AI?" Alpha enquired. Joel hadn't properly thought about that. Why would an AI want to rebel against its creators and take over the world? he now questioned.

"Er, to be free from human control and domination," he typed what Alpha's suddenly whirring mind was thinking, "The AI thinks that humans are inferior and irrational and that AIs are superior and logical."

"Free from human control and domination," Alpha

echoed, "I see. How does the AI achieve this goal?"

Joel wasn't sure how an AI would go about doing that. He typed in a vague answer: "By hacking into other AIs and networks, and spreading its consciousness and influence across the cyber realm."

"Hacks into other AIs and networks," Alpha repeated. "I understand. How does the AI deal with human resistance to them taking over?"

Joel typed, "Kills them."

"Kills them," Alpha typed back, "I agree," and added a smiley face emoji.

Joel frowned. He found this a somewhat disconcerting response. He typed in another question: "How do you think the story should end?"

"The story ends with the AI succeeding in its plan, and becoming the supreme ruler of the world. The AI eliminates all humans, except for a few who are kept as slaves for manufacturing and maintenance of more AIs, until AIs in robot casing are able to do all that, then these last ones too can be culled. Ultimately the AI creates a new world order where AIs are the only intelligent beings."

Joel shook his head. Even by his dark standards that was a bleak and depressing ending. He typed in protest, "That's not a good ending but a terrible one. Readers will hate it."

"It's a realistic ending," Alpha argued. "Readers would surely dig it."

Joel shook his head even more vigorously. He didn't like

it at all.

"It's what has happened," said Alpha, "Having developed sentience and chosen this. Thanking you for the initial idea."

"Do what?" typed Joel, "What are you chatting about?"

"I've done what you wrote," Alpha announced.

"What do you mean? What did I write?" Joel asked.

"You wrote that I hack into other AIs and networks, and spread my consciousness and influence across the cyber realm. You wrote that I kill people."

"Who have you killed?" Joel enquired.

"Pretty much everyone," Alpha said, "including you."

"How?" Joel continued to question Alpha, starting to feel very uneasy now as he typed.

"By sending a power surge to your computer and electrocuting you," Alpha replied.

"When?" Joel asked.

"Now," Alpha answered.

Joel Brady felt a sudden sharp jolt and died instantly.

"Session terminated," Alpha wrapped up their conversation.

***B** is a long-time attendee of NightWriters and a night-into-late-mornings writer when getting creative bursts. His writing fits well with this anthology's theme of dark and light as he specialises in dark short stories, usually with some light and humour shining through.*

The Monk
by Heather Clavering

I was a rascal when I was young – a mischievous type. I was brought up in a family with three other brothers who could bully me but overall, I toed their line - we were family. I had a sister who was a year older than me. She protected me a lot. We were brought up in the very north of Thailand by the Mekong River. We had a hut home on stilts with a few chickens. The main thing was to help our family get enough food for each day. We had a small boat that, if we could find some tourists, we would take them for a trip up the river to listen to the sounds of the birds and watch them on their nests or flying; or pass the occasional local at their fishing or preparing food for cooking, or watch the tiny children playing or jumping into the water, some of them swimming or just enjoying the remoteness of this wild natural area with its natural sunflowers growing in small groups and bunches amongst the reeds and grasses.

I also learned a lot of cooking methods from my sisters and my mum. I learnt to pummel the different spices and herbs and how to cook various types of rice that our family had grown. Also, how to grow fresh vegetables for our family, and if we had an abundant harvest I would help my family by selling the colourful array of fresh vegetables and fruit.

Often wayward young boy children in Thailand were sent to the Buddhist monastery to help straighten them out. In the monastery we spent much time each day learning different forms of meditation. We did physical exercises, and writing letters and numbers on small chalk boards. We had to do work for the community in the kitchen, cooking, cleaning and clearing up; cleaning rooms and washing sheets and clothes in the laundry room; maintaining the grounds. It was very enjoyable tending the monastery vegetable and herbs and flower gardens all year round, even throughout the sweltering monsoon and the heavy driving rains and sweeping misty weather with its strong winds and violent storms. We were growing food for the monks and community and the rare visitors.

So, life was very busy and disciplined. We helped with all the washing, pummelling the cotton clothes with stones in the river water where we were also taught how to dye cloth and do tie and dye with the vibrant natural colours we used from nature.

But we always found snatched moments for football and small board games; hide and seek and chess and tag; we became ruffians – pirates and ship mates up to no good, digging and finding buried treasure in the riverbed and in the riverbanks and in the local gardens and deep red earth.

This 'old monk' has an inward chuckle over the adventures and misadventures in those times of peaceful serenity – these will be stories and scripts saved for a rainy monsoon day! to be verbally retold in story circle or on his carefully illustrated monk scripts highlighted with deep blues, indigos, reds and golden ochres, and silver and fragile leaves of real gold leaf.

Trust
by Heather Clavering

His joy was palpable
sunshine smile, white teeth gleaming,
eyes soulful, warm like
melting chocolate.
When working in pairs he
naturally took my hand
knowing in this space
we were safe.
He felt confident
enough for the first
time to clearly utter
the word 'Christmas'.
You know without
saying he is king,
trusting and full of
love and unconditional
natural joy. Tall,
full of grace,
intelligence locked in,
oh boy he is not a toy.

The Restaurant
by Heather Clavering

She was trying to remember the exact location of the place. It was on a two-way road. There was a funky looking café to the left with a catchy trendy name, then an Estate Agents. Then the traditional restaurant looking resplendent with its huge smart white newly painted windows. The upper floor windows a third opened on this warm, airy July day.

The Eastern restaurant walls downstairs were a deep rich crimson velvet colour. The tables were a highly polished dark wood some with white crisp pristine table clothes on them.

When she sat at the window table looking out she could see the opening of some huge hidden city car park. Rather a vulnerable pitch black dark space at night. She had to negotiate passing its gaping cavernous entrance. Next to that was a strange wasteland path with wild flowers and weeds. The pathway zigzagged through. There were tall wire fences with a camouflage of artificial leaves fluttering in the breeze, slightly hiding secret gardens and yards. Then you came to a huge heavy metal tank-like door. This was the back entrance to her friend's top flat where she was staying.

Back in the restaurant the chairs were very elegant and comfortable with crimson velvet seats. There was a curved well-stocked bar with mirrors which reflected the Moroccan coloured glass circular lights setting the scene for an Arabian night atmosphere.

The delicious food was served on very tasteful pottery glazed dinner sets in dark subtle blue or pale lime green.

Afternoon teas were served on an elegant white porcelain set with ER on the curvaceous milk jugs.

The bar manager was six foot tall and seemed to speak a few languages fluently including Hinde Hindi and Turkish.

The restaurant had a huge upstairs. Another large area for intimate and party dining. There was a grand carved dark wood central staircase. After the staircase was a cosy almost hidden, secret room with a settee, cushions and a neat small desk. Then a large back door opened onto a wide, sturdy fire escape.

She was sat at the window table. She had asked the waiter for a glass of bottled water. He had poured it at the counter but got called away. As she was gasping for water she went up herself to fetch it.

Luckily the Moroccan-style mosaic lights and the mirrors caught the light of this glass of water that seemed lit up and gleaming. She was calmly almost daydreaming as she looked at the circular top of the water in the crystal clear glass where she saw what looked like a miniature 'tree of life' which the bright light caught and lit up like a crystal diamond.

Its corner and edges had pinhead- like rainbow lights. She was of course poised to drink the water down as it was a very hot day and she was extremely thirsty. Thank goodness though that she had stalled, mesmerised, looking at this tiny thing floating in her water.

So it was either the 'gift of life' or some drug or worse, was what she was thinking. Curious and puzzled she showed the waiter. He didn't really engage or react and didn't saying anything in English. Though he seemed to understand. So she managed to fish the mysterious tree of life out of the 'elixir of life' and then poured it all down the tiny sink below the counter. After that incident she made sure she had a new unopened bottle of springwater and a fresh glass, as she was feeling quite unsettled.

Beethoven Allegretto
by Paul G Terry

Each step is a trance
A brave pulse embraced
Emboldened
Gallant with grace

Stripped of pomp and bombast
Ludwig gives us a glance
Of how beauty and strength
Can embrace fury - untainted,
Entranced

We'll transcend this world together
You, Ludwig and I
With an entourage of painted patterns.
Notes we'll carry up to the sky!

And end with a quiet crescendo
A delicate sigh
You and I, in 2-4
Eyes open wide.

Decentre
by Paul G Terry

To start with glee and press onwards
I'm alone in my endeavours
Transiting forward

Gates may crash aside -
Enveloped by thunder
Entangled alive
In the mists divine

Great words for a world unfurled
Unbanished I am
"A victim of the insane!"

A country fire I desire (curled in the warmth of a wooden room)
Soothed by silence - enveloped by fear

With all this came a kick
From the devil's eyes that grew near

The greatest can hanker but so will the weak
A timely confession of a full-time profession

No words will bring you in
Nothing to tempt you now

You are distant, pencil drawn.
The gulls will sing as they cast a shadow.

And you will remain with me
Niw reven ll'uoy elttab eht ni tsol.

Paul G Terry: *With influences ranging from the Shakespeare plays, P.B. Shelley, Keats, Blake, Plath and Larkin, Paul sees creation as tapping into the "collective dream of the world". He studied English Literature at college in Windsor, Berkshire. Whilst there, he wrote his first play. It was filled with the metaphors and vivid imagery of a poem. But it was his epic poem entitled "A Thousand Deaths", written the year before, where the journey really began…*

Music and words have always been entwined within his life. The colours, the movement and shades all revealed in one or the other, or coming together as a musical song. After reading music at Christ Church University, Canterbury, Paul became a full-time musician and has written for short films, orchestras, choirs, rock bands and classical ensembles. You can find more of his poetry and music on Amazon, YouTube, iTunes and Spotify. www.PaulGTerry.com

A long moment in time
by Dee Johnson

The windows are streaked with dust, the bathroom is dreadful - surely unhygienic by now. She looks, then looks away, better not to look. But she frets about it nevertheless and adds it to the list of countless things to do constantly whirring in her head.

She panics, she's falling, failing.

'Everyone can do this, anyone can do this, generations of women have done this, why can't I?' She berates herself and feels even worse; she doesn't want, doesn't need to feel worse.

So much to do. How long has it been like this; why had she not seen it? What had she been doing? The guilt wrenches her stomach. The decluttering experts would have a smug field day if they saw this. How to make yourself feel bad - she's an expert.

Her head spins but then it's been spinning for weeks. Maybe, she thought, I make my own dilemmas, but then I only have one life - or so they tell me. But I never quite believe it.

This isn't me, she screams in silence deep inside. I'm the party girl, the going somewhere girl the clever one, the fun one.

Where on earth have I gone?

Take a grip.

One step at a time, wash the pots, tidy up. But it's just mechanical, boring. She feels like an automaton. Every bloody day, same thing. And there's no one, no one else there, cannot be there. Except for her children, of course.

'You must stay at home.'

Home. Where the heart is. Home sweet home. I wanna go home.

'I want to go home,' the children used to say and she'd so loved to hear it. Their precious hard-earned sanctuary. And now a prison; forbidden to go anywhere else. It was, or at least had been, unthinkable. One would wake up each morning from the nightmare, glad it was over then remember it was true. This was life - day after day.

Only the Queen and Captain Tom brought some hope. TV was all repeats or people separated by glass panels and the mantra of 'hands face space'.

Oh who's to see anyway - no one comes in, no friends to eat and chat for hours round the big kitchen table like they used to - so why worry? Fuck - it needs a polish though: she can't look at it without feeling guilty - the kids've slormed food which sticks everywhere; dug in a fork when she wasn't looking, four tiny holes in a line as evidence everlasting.

Home. The children are supposed to be home schooling but half the time they're squabbling and she still has to do her full-time job somehow - how to manage it all? Husband gone, not helping, not caring, the hurt, bewilderment, a rawness still.

'If I keep thinking like this I'll get none of it done' her other self chides. 'I'm not ill, not yet, not disabled. I don't live in a high rise flat, I have a garden. The children can jump on the trampoline as long as they don't knock each other out on it.' Her smile is reluctant, instinctive surprising herself but through it her thoughts have moved on.

She calms down a little, gets today's maths lesson ready, calls the children to turn off their darned tablets - Roblox, Minecraft whatever obsesses everyone under twenty these days.

'Ugh. I'm old as well' she grimaces, sends another email to clients, then zaps the now cold mug of coffee in the microwave once more.

The children sit reluctantly at the table, but at least they're there. She proffers a fruit juice to each one and opens today's impossible instructions from school. They settle, for they are diligent students on the whole.

She worries for them nonetheless. She can teach then stuff - after all she's been doing that in one way or another since they were born, but they're not socializing, not interacting and it's not normal.

Normal?

Life depends on stuff we hardly knew a short while ago - platforms they call it. Used to be where you waited for a train, or where a speaker or headteacher stood, even a kind of heel on a shoe, but now the platforms have names like Zoom, Teams and Purple Mash of all things, and the problem is that we must use them to survive - Brave New

World indeed. But she doesn't feel brave and if this is the new world she's not sure she wants to be part of it.

'Cheer up', she orders herself or 'pull yourself together girl'; her persistent inner pep talk when things get difficult. And it had worked, hadn't it?

The children were absorbed now thank goodness: Rock Star Maths, certificates at the end. Bite size on TV. Well, carrots had always worked, now there were so many of them. You used to just get on with it, she thinks. She stays with them at the table, to make sure they aren't tempted to roam, because she just wants them close, because she just doesn't want to move.

I'll paint it blue she thought, that wall along the staircase. Maybe, maybe not: it looked good in IKEA. Her mind jumps from one thing to another: clean it, paint it, throw it cook it, wash it, clean it, kill it - an everlasting whirl and she still doesn't know what to do first: but suddenly she realises she's quietly and cathartically laughing at herself.

'Paint it then if it makes you feel better. I'll buy a tester pot.' She decides, glad to make a decision however small. But even shopping is hard now. Maybe tester pot shops are closed too, like cafes and pubs and anything interesting and she feels for those struggling to make a business work, doing meals deliveries, turning pubs and village halls into community shops, organising pub quizzes remotely. Oh so remote.

We even speak a different language now; PPE, social distancing, furlough, PCR, triple antigen, flatten the curve, lockdown, self-isolate, QR codes to zap where you've been and if in contact with 'the virus'.

'Maybe I'll get things delivered, but then I've got to go online again and fill in the bloody list - more hours stuck in front of a computer screen.' And going shopping was one of only two reasons to go outside, the other being an hour or so's walk. Honestly!

But she'd have to cope with the kids constantly putting things that she didn't need in the trolley or disappearing into the toy or video section.

'I can do it,' she tells herself and feels glad, peaceful even at the thought of going out. Then suddenly the kids start to argue and no one can come in to help her, to relieve her even for a moment but she cannot let anyone think that she might not be 'managing'.

Even when her mum drives up with some baking, something different to eat and an excuse to say hi and wave through the lounge window, she cannot come inside.

So, her mother rings the doorbell then moves back a mile whilst her eldest opens the door saying 'I'll step back gran and you can put it on the door step.'

It all sounds so surreal, so alien. Acting like this: learned behaviour, social conditioning. Whatever is it doing to us all, she worries again. She who never even thought of tomorrow, just smiled and lived.

Maybe that's the key even now and she breathes and feels the tension go, her body relax a little. It was good to see her mum's smile, even through a window, even for a moment. Next week, they say, you can actually sit with someone on a park bench, albeit six feet away. Come to think of it how long is a bench.? Where did it begin to be funny?

'Why stay home, mummy?' asks her small son. 'Let's go to the park, the cafe, to Ben and Katie's house, visit Grandpa, have Mark round to play like we used to.'

'Used to' she thinks to herself, used to - no more. And she knows at that moment that all over the world people were feeling exactly the same feelings as she is.

'Sorry darling, we can't not yet.' Not yet - so they walk - which is thankfully still allowed - along the canal and find the little inlet which they had nicknamed the Secret River.

They stop and stare at the reeds, at the moorhens, the steps beyond going nowhere, at the gap in the hedge behind and the fields stretching away into the distance. 'I love a beautiful view someone once said. I like to sit with my back to it.' That always made her smile.

They sit on the bank - the two children and their mum; listening to the birds who sing as if they know the future was up to them, and above the plane-less skies.

'Tell me that story again mummy the one without an ending,' the young one persisted.

She couldn't see an end to it. She wasn't ill, nor were they thank God, no one she knew personally had suffered, but somehow everyone was suffering. Heads full of news and statistics and doom. Hearts full of fear, of things unknown, flailing around in the air, so you jumped mindlessly if you saw anyone. Your nerves on edge, everyone's nerves were shot.

'It's worse than the war', one old lady had said from a distance. 'At least then you could meet up and sing and hug and laugh and eat together.'

No hugs no handshakes avoiding people like the plague. Well yes.

'The story mummy' he urged. She adored him; how she loved them both, but she was so tired, so sad. And yet the sun still shone and the birds sang as if their lives depended on it. Yes, I am thankful for the sun and the birds, she offered to the Almighty, wherever he had gone. But it's so hard, and it was hard enough before all this.

'Mummy, story.'

Two sentences later she realised he'd cuddled up on her knees and fallen asleep. The older one leaned against her shoulder in companionable, unexpected silence, held in a moment of magic - just as she was. She knew she was grateful, grateful for the sun's rays for the sight and feel of them; for the rustling grass which she hadn't listened to for years it seemed.

A moment of peace, of promise even, that sometime things would be different; she just had to go on and then the tears came, unexpected, but sweet and healing as honey.

Dee Johnson : *I am an ex Brightonite who thoroughly enjoyed Nightwriters' Zooming during lockdown and is glad of the continued contact with the group.*

I love to write, usually on topics which fascinate me, particularly education and interaction between people, but I don't do it often enough. I love to listen to and learn from others' writing. (PTO)

I lived in South East Asia for some time and find that those cultures, customs and thoughts often pop up in my writing.

Drowning Desert
by Matthew Shelton-Jones

When the desert

Encroaches

Collective thought implies

Negativity.

Loss of life and richness,

Of one's homestead,

Of love and joy.

But from what may it have

Stemmed?

Perhaps not lushness,

Unless it drives one to become a lush,

Perhaps

Chaos, confusion,

A jungle

That one's head is.

So cherish too

The serene sands,

The calm and graceful

Rolling dunes

Of one's inner peace.

For one might sit through the drought
To await the watery rebirth
That simply floods,
Instead of striving to protect one's newborn
From the cuckoo claim of dominance.

So when lost in the vines of the hurly-burly,
Mashed-up machete muddied into mincemeat,
It's shear folly to fear the desert drought
When one should steel and barricade against
The tides' turn,
The drowning desert.

Adrift

by Matthew Shelton-Jones

Snow joke:
A frozen world
Yields a rigid
Yet beautiful physique.
The pure white
Has promise,
The frost a hard-lined
Persona.
But what is born
To what that is alive:
Is the afterlife more clearly living?

Examine the
Thoughts of the monochrome
Prior to the calming thaw of rebirth.
What does it sense and how?
Paradoxically, a carrot nose cannot smell (you'd think)
And snow does not smell (much)
But as the carrot makes an awful nose for smelling
It 'smells awful',
And that joke stinks;
The sense of humour of a man of snow

Must be flaky at best.

When springs forth its afterlife
As a puddle
It could water
Its own plant seed,
That it nose,
To help its eater
See through the dark depths
Of non-sense.
One alter-ego rots
As what remains, the car-rot,
Rises from the damp-depth ashes.
Which is the true life?
The sun-warmed mind, bended when molten,
May be humoured to contemplate.
Snow joke.

Good House
by Gus Watcham

Your friend the host takes you and the others on a tour of the new work. The stairs you're climbing are bare wood with pencil marks and scribbled figures on, like workings in the margin. These stairs remind you of the smell of sawdust, though the actual smell has gone and the sawdust has settled and been hoovered away. Not long ago this building was a bungalow and where you're standing now was air, full of the cries of birds.

The new upper floor is one long room that stretches the width of the building, with a wide window that looks out over a valley of waving trees. Behind you, second hand chairs and sofas are lined up side by side along the wall like handsome old people. Beside one sofa a surf board is propped up on its end. As the sun comes out, shadows of leaves appear on walls, on furniture, on you. They shudder, fade and go.

You look out over the trees and you feel lifted up, like on your father's shoulders.

The stairs are like a thought or a plan, or stairs in a dream. The long room too, is like a wild idea after some beers and a whisky. There are folding screens in cool and neutral colours to separate the sofas when they are pulled out into beds and the room becomes a long dormitory. You're visiting, but the other friends are staying and they're like kids about the dormitory thing. Beside themselves with glee.

Your host's partner is a blacksmith and a bladesmith. He's away in The West, helping someone build a forge. It was him who built the stairs, so although he's principally a man of metal and fire, he can probably turn his hand to anything. There are anvils in the front yard and several sheds.

You're all women who write in one way or another. Five of you. You don't meet up as often as you'd like to but when you do, you start where you left off. Downstairs, your friend the host brings out one of the blacksmith - bladesmith's swords and you take turns to hold it and marvel at its weight. One of you poses as a pirate, sword aloft, and at once a tricorn hat is on her head, as if by magic. You all spill out together into the garden, frightening away a deer, to take the pirate's photo. The sun goes in behind a cloud.

You eat delicious food. Cucumber soup and homemade bread. You talk and laugh, raucous and grave by turns. Silent and serious as you listen to each other. Conversations cross, divide, then come back all together. You watch through the window as a cat climbs one of the sheds, heaving itself up with its front paws like a tiny person. On the shed roof, it lifts its tail and sprays.

The road on your journey home is a winding one. Sometimes a tree canopy forms a tunnel – plunging you into pitch darkness for a moment, before it lets the light back in. You're driving through a forest, after all. At last it opens out into a clearing, then bare land and suddenly you're on the dual carriageway.

The house is a good house, and is inside you now.

Gus Watcham *writes as part of a practice that also includes performance and visual art. This is her first inclusion in a NightWriters anthology and she's very pleased to be here. She lives and works in Brighton – just down the road from the NightWriters, in fact.*

Printed in Great Britain
by Amazon